TWO MEN, ONE BLADE

"We been lookin' for this here squaw," the stranger hissed. "This ain't your concern."

Clint lifted himself into a crouch, like a cobra rearing up from the bushes. He lunged forward, arms outstretched. His left hand grabbed for the stranger's knife hand, but the other man pulled it away. Clint's right hand got ahold of the stranger's jacket and his momentum took both men to the ground. But it was the stranger who hit the hardest. Both shoulders slammed into the dirt, driving a good portion of the breath from his lungs.

With a snap of his elbow, the stranger brought his arm around like a whip. His fist twisted along the way to bring the blade of his knife sailing toward Clint's throat. All Clint could do was pull back. The stranger's hand was coming too high to be blocked and too fast to be avoided. Clint felt the blade bite into his skin.

The stranger grinned at the sight of Clint's blood and brought his knife around to draw some more. But Clint managed to get his own arm in the way of the stranger's, so now it was a race to see who could move the fastest from there.

Once he was on his feet, the stranger put some more muscle behind his arm, demonstrating experience with his blade. An ugly smile grew on his face like an infection.

"I'll be takin' that squaw," the stranger grunted. "Whether you like it or not . . ."

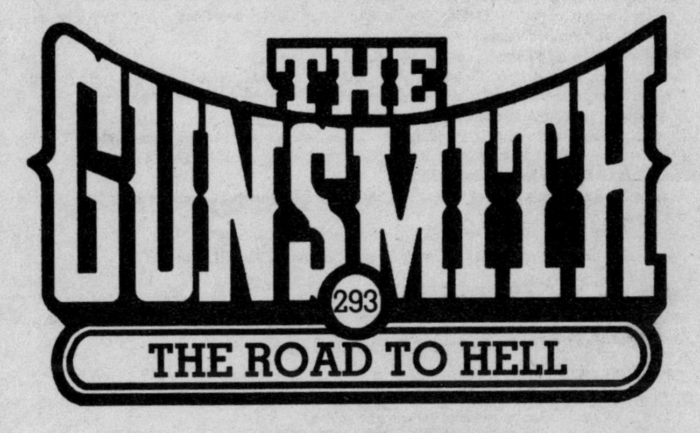

J. R. ROBERTS

JOVE BOOKS, NEW YORK

THE BERKLEY PUBLISHING GROUP
Published by the Penguin Group
Penguin Group (USA) Inc.
375 Hudson Street, New York, New York 10014, USA
Penguin Group (Canada), 90 Eglinton Avenue East, Suite 700, Toronto, Ontario M4P 2Y3, Canada
(a division of Pearson Penguin Canada Inc.)
Penguin Books Ltd., 80 Strand, London WC2R 0RL, England
Penguin Group Ireland, 25 St. Stephen's Green, Dublin 2, Ireland (a division of Penguin Books Ltd.)
Penguin Group (Australia), 250 Camberwell Road, Camberwell, Victoria 3124, Australia
(a division of Pearson Australia Group Pty. Ltd.)
Penguin Books India Pvt. Ltd., 11 Community Centre, Panchsheel Park, New Delhi—110 017, India
Penguin Group (NZ), Cnr. Airborne and Rosedale Roads, Albany, Auckland 1310, New Zealand
(a division of Pearson New Zealand Ltd.)
Penguin Books (South Africa) (Pty.) Ltd., 24 Sturdee Avenue, Rosebank, Johannesburg 2196,
South Africa

Penguin Books Ltd., Registered Offices: 80 Strand, London WC2R 0RL, England

THE ROAD TO HELL

A Jove Book / published by arrangement with the author

PRINTING HISTORY
Jove edition / May 2006

For information, address: The Berkley Publishing Group,
a division of Penguin Group (USA) Inc.,
375 Hudson Street, New York, New York 10014

ISBN: 0-515-14131-3

JOVE®
Jove Books are published by The Berkley Publishing Group,
a division of Penguin Group (USA) Inc.,
375 Hudson Street, New York, New York 10014.
JOVE is a registered trademark of Penguin Group (USA) Inc.
The "J" design is a trademark belonging to Penguin Group (USA) Inc.

PRINTED IN THE UNITED STATES OF AMERICA

10 9 8 7 6 5 4 3 2 1

ONE

When Clint tried to open his eyes, he thought his skull was about to split in half. The pain shot through him from back to front, sapping his strength and dropping him back onto a bed of straw.

"Aw, hell," Clint groaned as he reached up to press his fingers against his temple.

That movement hurt almost as much as the first, but he was able to lift his hand all the way up to his forehead. Considering how fast the barn was spinning around him and the queasiness in his belly, he thought he was doing pretty well.

Unfortunately, the few breaths he managed to pull in didn't help much. His legs were still as useless as limp noodles and his head was throbbing so badly that he could see blobs of dark red swelling in his vision in time to the pounding of his heart.

Rather than stand up all the way, Clint sat upright and stopped. He draped his arms over his knees and allowed his head to droop forward. For a few seconds, he kept his eyes shut so he could concentrate on breathing. It hurt, but he managed to take a few more breaths until he could finally fill his lungs.

He could hear some animals stirring nearby as well as a restless breeze coming in through a window with loose shutters. The banging wasn't more than a series of squeaks and taps, but those noises might as well have been shots from a cannon to his sensitive ears. Reluctantly, Clint fought the urge to cover his ears with his hands due to the effort it would have taken to lift his arms that far.

After the breeze had died down, Clint let out the breath he'd been holding and cracked one eye open. He could make out some shadows as well as just enough flickering light to realize that a lantern was hanging from a nearby wall.

He moved his legs and started to get up. When he did, his hands brushed up against loose straw and something solid to his left. It didn't take much for him to realize that he'd bumped against a bale of hay.

Moving was becoming easier the more Clint tried. The pain was still there, but at least Clint felt as if he could get to his feet without wanting to shoot himself to end his suffering. When he thought of that, his hand went reflexively to his holster.

The modified Colt was gone.

That realization snapped his eyes open quicker than being on the receiving end of a cold bucket of water.

What little light there was blazed into his eyes like a torrent of fire. After a few seconds of sharp pain, Clint managed to get his first real look at his surroundings. He was in a barn, sure enough, and it was a small one to boot.

A lantern hung on the wall behind him, barely illuminating the horse's stall he now occupied.

"At least that accounts for the smell in here," Clint muttered. Hearing his own voice filled his head with a painful jangling sound, but it faded quicker than the last batch of agony. At least this time, Clint managed to keep his eyes open until it passed.

Now that he had his wits more or less about him, Clint was determined to get to his feet and stop stumbling around like a fool. He grabbed hold of the bale of hay with one hand and hung onto the top of the stall with the other. From there, he managed to haul himself to his feet.

Just then, his eyes caught the glint of light off metal coming from a spot on the floor just outside his stall. Clint recognized the modified Colt's barrel instantly and staggered over to the fallen pistol. As he was reaching out to take hold of the gun, he caught sight of another pair of eyes staring at him from the shadows.

"Don't be afraid," Clint said softly. "You can come on out of there."

While gently picking up his gun and holstering it, Clint reached out with his other hand toward the set of wide, brown eyes.

After less than a second of hesitation, Eclipse stretched out his neck to rub his nose against Clint's fingers.

"That's it, boy," Clint said. "At least there's one friendly face in here. Now, I just need to remember where here is."

Just saying those words made Clint feel the full impact of what was happening. Although there were flickers in his mind of what had happened, there wasn't anything close to a full picture. Bits and pieces of the barn seemed familiar, but that might have been because most barns looked pretty much the same on the inside.

Eclipse took a few steps forward to meet Clint. The Darley Arabian stallion was a familiar sight and a very, very welcome one. Clint's hand wandered along the horse's mane, scratching his ears as he caught his breath.

The pounding in his head was still there, but wasn't as blinding as it had been a few moments ago.

His steps were becoming steadier the more he took, and

every breath he pulled into his lungs was giving him a little more energy.

Suddenly, Clint heard something moving. He turned toward the noise, even though he could tell it was coming from outside the barn. The door was nearly lost in the thick tangle of shadows along that wall, but his eyes were focused more upon the floor. In fact, when the door swung open, Clint hardly even noticed.

A man with long, greasy hair took one step into the barn and stopped. He gripped a hunting rifle, which he immediately swung to point in Clint's direction. "What's going on in here?" he asked. "Who the hell are you?"

Still looking at the shapes on the floor, Clint eventually shifted his eyes upward.

"I asked you a question, mister," the man in the doorway said.

"My name's Clint Adams. I just—"

"You're that gunfighter. That'd mean you were the one doing all the shooting."

"No, I . . ." Even as he said those words, Clint knew it would be a lie to say that he hadn't done any shooting. His head might have still been hurting, but a few of the bits and pieces in his head were already beginning to come together.

"You did this?" the man whispered as his eyes found the same shapes on the floor that Clint had been studying earlier.

This time, Clint didn't respond. Echoes flashed through his mind. Gunshots rattled through his brain and he recalled bodies twitching with pain before dropping to the floor.

They'd dropped to the floor to land in the quiet heaps that Clint and the other man had just discovered.

TWO

There were two of them that Clint could see. Their names were on the tip of his tongue, but retreated farther away from him the more he tried to recall them. One thing he could remember was the feel of his modified Colt bucking in his hand as he fired at least three times in a row.

"You killed these folks," the man whispered. Tightening his grip on his rifle, he took a reluctant half step backward while taking better aim at Clint. "You were the one doing all that shooting. You killed these two!"

"Look, I need to figure out what the hell went on here."

"I know what went on here. You're a killer and I ain't about to let you mosey off where you please."

Clint could see the other man's hands trembling. He knew he could draw his Colt and leave that barn any time he wanted. But there was already a mess of blood soaking into the straw covering the floor and Clint didn't want to spill any more just then.

"All right," Clint said as he raised his hands. "No need for the gun. I'm coming along nice and easy."

No matter how calmly Clint was speaking, the man with the rifle was only getting more shaky. "You make a move for that pistol and I'll pull my trigger!"

"I won't make a move for it. Just settle down."

Once the man was outside the barn again, he regained a bit of his composure. "Come out of there and be quick about it."

Clint did as he was told. As he stepped over the bodies, he tried to get as good a look at their faces as he could manage without upsetting his fidgety captor any more.

"I said come out of there!" the other man said.

When he was out of the barn, Clint felt a little better as well. Part of that was because of the cool night air, which washed over him to soothe the pains in his skull. Another part of that was the renewed hope he felt after having seen those bodies.

The details were still a bit shaky, but Clint knew that there was more than those two in the barn when the mess had started. Unless more bodies had been hidden somewhere, they were still able to move on their own.

"Hold up, mister," the man with the rifle ordered.

Clint couldn't help but get a bit nervous when the other man walked around to stand behind him. He could feel the rifle barrel was still pointed at him the way most folks could feel they were being watched. This time, that feeling was even more troubling.

"What are you doing?" Clint asked.

"Stand still or I'll shoot."

"I can try to explain what happened."

"Oh, you'll get yer chance for that."

"I'm not about to hurt anyone," Clint explained.

Just then, the modified Colt was snatched from Clint's holster and a series of quick, shuffling steps scurried around behind him. When the man with the rifle reappeared, he was tucking the Colt under his belt and smirking victoriously.

"You sure as hell won't hurt no one," the man declared. "Not no more."

"You could have just asked me to hand it over," Clint said.

"I ain't stupid. Now get moving."

Once more, the other man scurried around behind Clint so he could press the rifle barrel between Clint's shoulder blades. Even though Clint walked at a steady pace in the direction he was pointed, he still felt the occasional jab of the rifle knocking against his spine.

Actually, Clint was glad for the walk. It was a cool summer night and the stars were stretched out overhead like a glittering tapestry. The breeze did him a world of good and allowed him to clear his head and sort through some of the chaos rattling around in there.

Although there was a road under his boots, Clint knew he wasn't in a proper town. If he was, it wasn't much of one, closer to a large camp. Rickety homes were scattered here and there; not one of them leaning in the same direction as its neighbor.

It seemed as if there were some more buildings further along. Clint could see a few fires burning behind open windows and could hear some voices a little further away, which made him think the camp also had a saloon. That wasn't too far for his mind to leap, since most camps set up a saloon even before the blacksmith or doctor opened his doors.

With every breath of air he pulled into his lungs, Clint felt the fog in his head start to clear. There was still that chaos in there, but that was mostly due to the powerful pain that still thumped behind his eyes.

And just when Clint thought he was getting a handle on that chaos, another bunch of it came hurtling straight toward him.

Clint could make out at least four more men emerging from various houses. Only a couple of them appeared to be armed, but their weapons consisted of more hunting rifles or shotguns clutched in nervous hands.

"What you got there, Ed?"

"Found him in Abby's barn," the man with the rifle shouted over Clint's shoulder.

"He the one that did all the shooting?"

"That's what I aim to find out."

By this time, the number of men coming out to see what was going on had doubled. They formed a circle around Clint and Ed that was slowly tightening around them.

"What about the others that went into that barn?" one of the men asked. "Did they get away?"

"No," Ed replied. "They're dead."

Silence dropped down as if the sky had fallen. Slowly, nervous whispers began working their way through the crowd. It wasn't long before those whispers became restless and angry.

Up to now, Clint had been willing to keep quiet, let Ed do the talking, and see where this was headed. He was now getting a good idea of where it was headed, and he didn't much like it.

"Don't I deserve a chance to explain myself?" Clint asked.

Several of the onlookers shifted nervous eyes toward him, but didn't seem interested in what he had to say.

"If you give me a chance, I might just be able to shed some light on what went on in there," Clint said, doing his best to put some much-needed confidence into his voice. "Did anyone think of that, or are you just looking to spill some blood with no questions asked?"

"If you killed those people," the spokesman for the crowd said, "then I got no problem with burying you here and now and be done with it."

"And I suppose you know I did it?" Clint asked.

The man stepped forward to reveal a pockmarked face that was twisted into an angry scowl. Although that anger was easy enough to see, so was the fear lying just beneath it. "We all heard them shots, mister. The lot of you were seen walking into that barn and you're the only one that walks out. A goddamn mule could put them pieces together."

As much as he hated to admit it, Clint couldn't argue with that logic. "I'm not the only one who made it out of there."

A few people gasped, but most of them either kept quiet or whispered some more amongst themselves.

"That true, Ed?" the pockmarked man asked.

"I saw the bodies, Art. You want to go in there and see for yourself, go right ahead. I don't want to set foot in that barn again."

Clint studied Art's pockmarked face. The effort of thinking seemed to be putting a mighty strain upon him. Finally, Art spit and shook his head.

"To hell with it," Art grunted as he lifted his shotgun. "I say we bury this asshole in the same hole as them others he killed. At least that'll be the end of it."

Although a few of the others in the crowd weren't of the same mind as Art, nobody there was about to lift a finger against him.

THREE

Clint glanced around expectantly at the crowd. He wasn't quite sure what he was expecting, but it was a whole lot more than what he got. Those who didn't look away from him outright, stared back as if he was the Devil incarnate.

Art lifted his shotgun to his shoulder and sighted down the barrel. It was that moment when Clint knew he had only two choices: fight or die.

The choice between those two was made in half a heartbeat. In a blur of motion, Clint brought up his right arm and turned sharply in that direction. Even before he saw the rifle in Ed's hands, he felt his forearm knock against its barrel. Clint kept turning on the balls of his feet until he was standing at Ed's side.

With his right hand, Clint grabbed hold of the rifle barrel and forced it upward. With his left, he pulled the rifle out of Ed's grip completely. The moment he felt the gun come free, Clint hopped into the clear.

"There's no need for this!" Clint shouted. "I barely even rem—"

But Clint was cut off by a flood of angry voices coming in from every direction. While plenty of the onlookers had been happy to let Art take aim and execute Clint on the spot, they weren't going to stand for Clint speaking another word in his own defense.

"Kill him!" Someone screamed.

"Shoot before *he* does!"

"He's a mad dog!"

Nodding solemnly, Art steeled himself and tightened his finger around his trigger.

There came the blast of gunfire, which caused everyone in the crowd to jump. Nobody jumped higher than Art, however, since he was the one who felt a bullet drill into the earth no more than a few inches from his left foot.

Ed's gun was smoking in Clint's hands. As much as he wanted to press his advantage, Clint forced himself to keep the rifle aimed at the hole he'd just shot into the ground.

"I'll come along and do my best to cooperate," Clint warned, "but I won't allow myself to be executed for murders I didn't commit."

"Then who did kill them folks?" Art asked. "What the hell went on in there?"

"Since everyone here just wants my blood, I won't do my talking out here. I'll say what I have to say to someone who's willing to listen. Where's the law around here?"

"We take care of our own selves, mister," Ed explained. "Otherwise, I wouldn't have bothered with any of this."

"Yer damn right," Art growled. "We take care of ourselves, which is exactly what I aim to do."

Clint could read Art's intentions as clearly as if they'd been written across his forehead. Unfortunately, they were pretty much the same as the last time he'd pointed his shotgun in Clint's direction.

Since Clint hadn't loaded the rifle, he couldn't be certain how many shots were still left inside it. But it was something more than that which made him reluctant to pull his trigger. Needless to say, he didn't bother explaining himself to any of the unsympathetic souls scowling at him at that moment. Instead, Clint did the next best thing he could come up with.

Turning the rifle as if he was presenting it to Art, Clint snapped both arms forward and launched the rifle through the air. Art's first impulse was to recoil and turn his head, which wasn't much help once the rifle barrel smacked against his chin.

Before the rifle had a chance to hit the ground after bouncing off Art's face, Clint was right there to reclaim it. Not only did Clint pluck the rifle from the air, but he also managed to snatch the shotgun from Art's hand as well.

Judging by the way Art folded into a ball and covered his head with both arms, he fully expected to get shot by one or both of the weapons Clint had taken.

Although he wasn't going to kill Art or anyone else at the moment, Clint suddenly realized that he might be forced to do something just as drastic. The folks in the crowd who hadn't run for cover were sighting down their own weapons with scared, panicked eyes.

A shotgun blast tore through the night, followed by another. Since neither Clint nor anyone else from the crowd had fired those shots, everyone looked around to see who did.

"You all should be ashamed of yourselves!"

A woman stepped forward with shotgun in hand. Even as she glared at the crowd, her hands quickly reloaded the weapon and snapped it shut. She was tall and slender, with skin that even looked tanned in the pale moonlight. Long, thick brown hair flowed over her shoulders and rustled in front of her face.

She came over to stand by Clint while keeping the shotgun moving toward the members of the crowd. "What in the hell is happening here?" she demanded.

Art jumped to his feet as if to reclaim the dignity he'd lost on his way down. "We're putting a killer to death!"

"Clint's no killer. Plenty of you should know that!"

"He's a gunfighter, Abby. Everyone knows that much."

"And you're a loudmouthed coward," Abby replied. "Why should I pick you over him?"

A few snickers came from the crowd. Seeing the flustered look on Art's face seemed to be more than enough to cause a few more.

"Everyone clear out of here," Abby said. "We tend to our own matters, so I'll take Mr. Adams here into my home. Anyone here think I can't handle myself well enough for the job?"

"Better than Art could," somebody snickered.

There were plenty of other comments passed around. Most of them ranged from "Let her have him, serves her right," to ". . . can always come back to finish the job."

"Come on, Clint," Abby said. "There's been more than enough excitement for one night. If it's all the same to you, it might be a good idea if you—"

Clint handed her his guns before Abby even finished her request.

FOUR

The door was barely closed when Abby set her shotgun down and turned to face Clint. Before he could get a word out, he was nearly knocked back outside when she rushed into his arms. Clint barely able to steady himself amid a flurry of kisses and a powerful hug.

"I'm so glad you're alive," she said when she took a breath. "After all that was happening"—she paused to kiss him several times on the cheeks—"after hearing those shots"—she paused again to kiss him on the lips—"I was starting to fear the worst."

Clint started to speak, but was cut short by a sharp jab of pain from the back of his head.

"Oh, no," Abby said as she pulled back from him. "You're hurt."

Now that she'd moved back a little, Clint was able to see the blood on Abby's fingers. She'd just been sliding her fingers through his hair, only to find them covered in blood. "What happened to you?"

Clint let out a breath and walked away from the door.

The inside of Abby's house was the most familiar thing he'd seen since spotting Eclipse inside that barn. The little two-room home was a bit cluttered, but was quiet and filled with the smells of dinner. Well, burnt dinner anyway.

Black smoke rose from a stew pot on top of a nearby stove. When she saw that, Abby hurried over to the kitchen. "Sit down, Clint," she said in a rush. "I was in the middle of cooking when I heard all those voices."

Sitting down on that rickety little chair felt better than if Clint had found himself resting on a throne made of gold. He let out a long, satisfied groan and started rubbing his eyes.

"Are you all right?" Abby asked anxiously. "What was that sound?"

"It was me taking a breath," Clint replied. "Nothing more."

"Where did that blood come from?"

Tentatively, Clint reached around to feel the sore spot on the back of his head. Sure enough, when he touched the bloody patch back there, the throbbing in his skull exploded into something that took away the breath he'd just taken.

"Just a knock on my head," Clint replied through a wince. "You have any water around here?"

After taking the stew pot off the stove and setting it to one side, Abby rushed over to a pitcher and dipped a rag into it. "Here," she said while making her way back to Clint. "Let's get you cleaned up a bit."

When he felt the cool touch of the rag against the back of his head, Clint did his best not to squirm or let out the profanities that were springing fluidly to mind.

"Does that hurt?" she asked.

Clint forced a smile onto his face and replied, "No. Not at all."

"Good. Maybe you can tell me how you got this nasty bump on your head while I fetch some bandages."

"That's the problem," Clint said. "I can't tell you very much."

"Don't you trust me?"

"It's not that. I seem to be having a hard time remembering."

Abby had been leaning over Clint so she could reach around and dab the wet cloth against his head. When she heard him say that, her brown eyes widened and she pulled in a quick breath. "Oh, my Lord. I knew someone who lost their memory. He was in the war and he was grazed in the temple by a bullet."

Clint shook his head. "It's nothing that bad. It's more like the last few hours are just . . . faded."

Although that calmed her down a little, Abby was still frowning as she took the cloth away from Clint's head so she could wring it out over the washbasin. "Faded?"

"Yeah. Actually, it may be more than a few hours. It's kind of hard to tell. I'm feeling better already, though, so I know it can't be anything too serious."

While Clint was talking, Abby had busied herself with something in the other room. After no more than a few seconds, she came out with a small box in her hands. It was a small, dented tin box that squeaked a bit when it was opened.

"What's the last thing you remember?" she asked.

"Let's see. I think I recall you leaving the room."

"Very funny. Keep that up and I'll be laughing while I'm stitching you back together."

"Wait a second. Stitches? I thought you said you were going to find some bandages."

Abby held up a small roll of bandages that had been tucked under one arm. "And here they are."

"What's in the box?" Clint asked.

"My sewing kit."

"Christ."

Abby giggled as she pulled up a chair so she could sit

behind Clint. "Don't tell me the big and terrible Gunsmith is afraid of a needle."

"I'm not afraid of fishing hooks either," Clint replied. "But that doesn't mean I want you to jab one of those through the back of my head."

"There are as many good doctors around here as there are lawmen. That means we have to take care of more than just our own legal matters."

Before he could say another word, Clint felt a slight pinch in the back of his head. It made him wince, but wasn't much when compared to the constant throbbing that filled the greater portion of his skull.

Abby worked quickly and skillfully, closing up the wound on the back of Clint's head in no time at all. Soon, she was once again dabbing at him with a wet rag and fussing at him with a hand towel.

"There now," she said soothingly. "That wasn't so bad, was it?"

While reaching out to wrap his arm around her waist, Clint said, "I can think of better ways to spend our time together."

At first, Abby put up a bit of a struggle. While she responded just fine to the way Clint touched her, she was having trouble getting herself to touch him. "I don't want to hurt you, Clint."

"After what I've been through, there's not much else for you to do that would be any worse."

Stepping away from him, Abby pulled the ribbon that closed the front of her blouse until it came completely free. The garment opened just enough to give him an enticing view of her full, pendulous breasts. "Then how about if I try to make you feel all better?"

FIVE

Clint slipped his hands inside her open blouse so he could cup Abby's breasts. They filled his hands and then some. Her nipples grew hard against his palms with just a little bit of movement on his part. Although she kept fairly quiet, he could hear the contented purr coming from the back of her throat. He could even feel it a bit as he moved his hands over her body.

"I take it this means you remember who I am," Abby said as she slipped out of her blouse and let Clint pull her closer.

"You're the prettiest woman in the Montana Territory and awfully handy with a shotgun."

"I'm serious, Clint. You didn't look like yourself when I spotted you in that mob. There was even a dazed look in your eyes all the way until I started in on your stitches."

"I guess there's something about getting your scalp sewed back on that tends to wake a man up."

Hiking up her skirt a bit, Abby climbed onto Clint's lap. She swung one slender, shapely leg around so she could straddle him and then set herself down. After a few shrugs of her shoulders, the blouse dropped off her and fell to the floor.

"Does this bring back some memories?" she asked softly.

Clint ran his hands along her thighs and then up to her hips. Abby's skirt bunched up under his hands, but he found his way underneath it soon enough. "Sure does."

"Like what?"

"Like how I've been wanting to do this since the moment you brought me back here."

"I'm serious, Clint. Tell me what you remember."

"Is this a test?"

Abby pressed her hands flat against Clint's chest. Part of that was so she could feel the muscles under his shirt, while another part was to keep them from getting too much closer than they already were. "Maybe it is a test. That's a pretty bad gash on the back of your head."

Letting out a sigh, Clint rubbed his hands up and down Abby's sides as he told her, "I remember riding into town a week or so ago."

"What's the name of this town?"

Clint started to roll his eyes, but managed to keep his patience intact. "Sharps. The town's name is Sharps."

When she heard that, Abby slid her hands along Clint's arms so she could guide his hands over her body. As she felt Clint's palms slide over her sides and brush slowly against her breasts, Abby curled her full, red lips into a naughty smile.

"I like this game," Clint said. The longer his hands remained on her body, the harder his erection became. Abby positioned herself on top of him so she could rub against the growing bulge in his jeans.

"You ready for the next question?" she asked.

"More than you could know."

"When was the first time we met?"

"A few months ago," Clint replied. "I stopped by on my way up to Canada."

Nodding slowly, Abby guided Clint's hands back over her breasts so they could come to a stop at a spot low upon her hips. "And what were you doing in town the most recent time you were here?"

"I was meeting up with Mason Barnes."

She moved his hands a bit lower. After all the rustling she'd done in his lap, Abby's skirt was hiked up to her waist in the front and draped behind her to completely cover Clint's legs. That way, as Clint's hands moved lower, he felt nothing but silky smooth skin and the slightest hint of lace.

"And who's Mason Barnes?"

"Do we really need to talk about him?" Clint asked as he moved his hands a little lower.

Abby locked her gaze directly onto Clint's eyes. The longer she focused her stare on him, the fuller her smile became. "You look a lot better than when you were outside."

"I'm feeling a lot better."

"Why were you stumbling around like that, Clint? I was getting scared just watching you."

"I took a knock on the head," Clint said as he slipped his hands around to the inside of her thighs. From there, he began rubbing slowly so his fingers could occasionally slide over the warm spot between her legs.

"Do you know how you got that knock?"

Forcing himself to concentrate on anything but Abby right then would have been a challenge under any circumstances. In fact, she was more of a distraction than anything else since the fog had all but lifted from his brain.

Finally, Clint shook his head. "Someone hit me. That's all I can say for certain."

Abby studied his face until she saw enough to ease her own mind. "Well, I'm just glad you're back to your normal self. That is, you're back as far as I can tell."

"I should be fine until that mob decides to knock down your door."

Now, it was Abby who let her hands explore Clint's body. She rubbed his shoulders and worked her way down along his chest. "They won't."

"Can you be certain of that?"

She nodded. "If they were going to do anything drastic, they would have done it while you were right there in the middle of them. Enough of those folks know how hot-headed Art can be, but I doubt anyone will do much of anything unless they heard anything suspicious coming from in here."

"Suspicious, huh?" Clint asked as he slipped his hand beneath her panties. While rubbing the moist lips of her vagina, he added, "You mean like shots?"

"Or screaming," Abby gasped.

"Then we'll have to keep quiet."

Leaning back and shuddering as she felt Clint rub the sensitive skin of her clitoris, Abby whispered, "I can't make any promises."

SIX

It didn't take long before Abby was tugging at Clint's belt and pulling open his pants. After a bit of squirming from the both of them, she was able to reach into his jeans and wrap her fingers around his stiff penis. While Clint pulled her panties to one side, she guided him into her and finally lowered herself down.

Letting out a slow breath as she impaled herself on him, Abby didn't stop moving until Clint was all the way inside her. Her eyes were wide and she tightened her arms around his neck.

Clint placed his hands upon her hips and held on as he began pumping in and out of her. Soon, Clint was leaning back against his chair and quickening his pace with every thrust.

"Oh, God," Abby breathed. "That's it right there."

Grabbing onto the back of the chair, Abby started riding Clint with a rhythm of her own. Her legs draped down on either side and her hips were pumping back and forth in short, quick motions.

As she rode him, Clint moved his hands over her breasts. He cupped them and squeezed when he was all the way inside her, which caused Abby to close her eyes and moan appreciatively. The moment she caught herself making a noise, she bit down on her lower lip. She did not, however, have any intention of stopping what she was doing.

Clint found one of her sweet spots as he angled his hips a certain way and thrust into her. Abby responded with a little yelp and opened her eyes in surprise. Before she could do anything else, he pumped into her again and immediately felt her body respond.

Abby's body started to tremble and she grabbed onto the chair as if her life depended on it. Although she struggled to keep herself from crying out, her hips were grinding desperately against Clint's. She couldn't seem to get him inside her fast enough, and every time he pumped his hips forward, she tensed a little bit more.

Clint thrust into her again and again, until he could feel Abby's climax working its way under her skin. As she was in the grip of her orgasm, Clint stood up and carried her along with him. He stayed inside her as he got up from the chair, cupping her buttocks in both hands.

When she saw that she was being lifted up, Abby started to smile. Clint thrust powerfully into her and pushed her straight into another orgasm. Her pussy tightened around him and he could feel her becoming even wetter between her legs. It was a few moments before he could set her down without her knees giving out beneath her.

Once she was able to stand, Abby gathered up her skirts and shifted them so they were bunched up at her side rather than at the back. Bending so she was leaning over the chair, she arched her back and held on while looking at Clint over her shoulder.

From where Clint was standing, he was able to see the perfect curve of Abby's lower back as it sloped down into her rounded buttocks. All of that was framed by her skirts, which were now pulled aside like a curtain for him.

Clint positioned himself behind her and rested one hand on her hip. With the other, he guided his cock into her as she spread her legs apart a bit more to accommodate him. He slid easily into her, and didn't stop until he was all the way inside.

Abby kept her eyes on Clint. It was easy enough to read the intensity on her face as she fought to keep her moans down to a minimum. That effort became even more difficult as Clint took hold of her hips with both hands and began thrusting in earnest.

His cock plunged deeply into her. Their bodies met in a steady rhythm that grew faster and faster.

Abby's knuckles turned white as she held onto the chair. Despite her efforts, her satisfied groans could still be heard as they were drawn out from the back of her throat. In a matter of minutes, she let out a loud breath and trembled with pleasure.

Clint might have eased up a bit just to make it easier for Abby to maintain her self-imposed vow of silence, but he wasn't thinking about that just then. Instead, he was more focused on how easily he slid in and out between her slick, smooth lips.

The feel of her hips in his hands, combined with the way her long hair draped across her back, made him even harder. When he saw her straighten her back just enough for him to get a good look at her proud breasts, he gave in completely to his own desires.

He thrust powerfully into her, and Abby responded with another moan.

Pulling out, Clint was only able to give himself a second or two before plunging straight back into her. When he did, he exploded with his own climax and nearly felt as dizzy as he had when he'd first opened his eyes in that barn not too long ago.

Abby struggled to catch her breath. Her eyes were wide as saucers as the last bit of her orgasm swept through her. Once the intense feelings settled down a bit, she tossed her hair to one side and took another look back at Clint.

"Oh, my . . . oh, my God," she whispered.

Pulling in a few haggard breaths of his own, Clint stepped back and lowered himself onto another one of the nearby chairs. "Yeah," he breathed. "That's just what I was thinking."

Abby was hastily pulling her clothes back into place and doing her best to straighten her skirts. All the while, she never took her eyes off Clint. When she'd somewhat collected herself, she walked over to him and eased herself onto his lap.

"Now that," she said, "is the Clint Adams I remember."

"Glad you approve."

"Now, are you going to tell me what else happened to land you in that barn? The last I heard, you and Mason were headed into Oregon."

"I'll tell you the whole story, just as soon as I catch my breath."

Once Clint was dressed, he started talking. . . .

SEVEN

Three Weeks Earlier

It was the middle of summer and the days were so bright that the sun was nearly blinding as it reflected off the streams that wound their way through northern Wyoming. Clint had ridden there to look in on a friend who seemed to have dropped off the face of the earth.

Mason Barnes was a good man, but had a weakness for any sort of gambling. He'd won enough money to settle down several times over, but had lost all of it and then some in the same amount of time. In the end, like most gamblers, Mason found himself just short of even.

This time, however, it seemed he'd fallen even shorter than usual.

After visiting dozens of rat-infested saloons and talking to more scowling cardsharps than he could count, Clint had managed to pick up Mason's trail. It led straight to the Holdout Saloon in a town called Especial.

So far, Clint couldn't find anything special about it.

The hills were green and rolled out to the north of Especial in a still wave. The heat in the air was tempered by the breeze blowing in from the west. Even all of that couldn't do much to make the town look like anything more than a few dirty bumps in a perfectly good road.

By the looks of it, the buildings on either side of the street had either weathered more than their share of storms, or had been cobbled together from pieces of less fortunate structures. The street was a crooked row of turned earth, rutted and studded with rocks jutting up at odd angles. As he walked along, Eclipse let out some discontented snorts aimed back at his rider.

"I know," Clint said as he patted the Darley Arabian's neck. "It's been a long ride. Soon as I find a suitable place, you can have a rest and some food. Sound good?"

Either the stallion wasn't impressed by Clint's promises, or he was still too perturbed at the beating his hooves were taking. Either way, Eclipse kept grumbling until he was led to a shady stall in a large shack.

"I don't want to hear a thing from you," Clint said as he removed Eclipse's saddle and scooped some oats into a bucket. "By the looks of it, this might be the best room in town."

On the way to the Holdout Saloon, Clint realized just how true his last statement was. Folks of all shapes and sizes were coming out to walk the streets or just get a look at who was walking by. Working girls sat straddling the posts of upper-floor balconies, displaying their wares without much concern for subtlety. They hollered down to the men on the street and most of those men hooted right back. Before Clint made it to the next corner, a stagecoach rattled into town, forcing him to jump to the side of the street.

It was getting rowdy in Especial, so Clint decided to step up his efforts to find the Holdout before everyone else did.

The place looked like an old general store. It had the wide front window and spacious porch normally used to display goods, but the only things on display were men who had been kicked out or were too drunk to get back in.

A cloth banner hung over the door, telling Clint that he'd found the right place in large, red painted letters.

When he stepped through the narrow front door, Clint's initial suspicions were confirmed. A counter was placed directly to his right, complete with a rusty cash register. He could almost picture candy on the little shelves built into the front of the counter, even though they were currently filled with snuff boxes and cheap cigars.

It was fairly early in the evening, but the Holdout was already packed full. A few more working girls made their rounds while another two ladies kicked up their heels upon a stage nailed together from old crates. They were accompanied by two men playing a harmonica and banjo whose talent was overshadowed by their enthusiasm to make noise. In addition to that, the men who weren't shouting to each other were singing along to the deafening music.

The counter had an addition sloppily tacked onto it that stretched an additional five or six feet. Standing behind that was a tall man with sharp eyes and dark skin. His features appeared more Spanish than Mexican, but his accent was a blend of several others.

"What you want?" the bartender snarled.

With all the ruckus going on inside the Holdout, Clint barely was able to make out those words. He tried to answer a few times, but was only met by a shake of the barkeep's head. Finally, Clint raised his voice and chopped his own sentence to its barest essentials.

"Mason Barnes," Clint said. "Need to see him."

"Gonna pay his debt?"

"Just want to talk."

Rather than shout over the voices of a few drunks stumbling in off the street, the barkeep jabbed his finger toward the back of the room. Clint tipped his hat in appreciation and started to walk away. He made it about one step before he felt a hand clamp around his arm.

Clint's first instinct was to turn and look at the barkeep, who was now leaning forward over the counter.

The dark-skinned man didn't react in the slightest to the fire in Clint's eyes. Instead, he said, "Nobody goes in that don't drink."

"I'll have a beer."

Despite the scowl that had been on his face moments ago, the barkeep gave Clint a friendly nod as he handed him a glass filled with a cloudy, foamy brew. After that, the barkeep aimed his glare at the next set of men trying to sneak past him without buying drinks.

Clint sipped the beer as he maneuvered his way through the saloon. It had been a while since he'd seen Mason Barnes, but the last time he had was in a dump only slightly worse than the Holdout. With so many bodies packed into one space and milling about like choppy waters, Clint started to wonder if he would ever find Barnes.

Once he heard the sound of a fist smacking against a jawbone, he knew he was in the right place.

EIGHT

"You'll pay for that, you son of a bitch!"

Those words echoed through the Holdout Saloon like thunder. The moment the fight had started, almost everything else in the place came to a stop. Folks backed off to give the brawlers some room as well as to get themselves out of harm's way. Everyone else seemed to be enjoying the show.

The man who'd just spoken was a tall Cherokee with thick black hair tied back into a tail that hung midway down his back. There were small beads and gold chips threaded into his mane, adding more than a little sparkle as he stumbled backward into a table.

"You talk a good game," a burly redheaded man shot back. "Let's see if you got more than just steam to back it up."

The second fellow stood just over six feet tall and looked as if he'd just been invited to dance. He kept his meaty fists balled up in front of him and his eyes fixed upon the Cherokee. Thick red hair was matted in clumps and stuck to his head. The clothes he wore were almost as bad and were stained with at least a few weeks' worth of dirt and sweat.

"Walk away from this now," the Cherokee said. "Otherwise, you'll get hurt."

The other man shook his head as the smile on his face grew even wider. "Why walk away now? This thing just got started." With that, he gritted his teeth and stepped forward with a powerful left hook.

Having already tasted the redhead's punching power, the Cherokee was quick to step out of the way of the next incoming fist. As that punch sailed past his head, the Cherokee delivered a chopping right uppercut to the redhead's side. The impact made a dull thump that even caused some of the onlookers to wince.

To his credit, the redhead barely flinched. After flicking out a left jab, he cocked back his right arm and sent it to catch the Cherokee's face in mid-duck. Sure enough, that first punch set the Indian up perfectly for the second.

"All you injuns fight the same," the redhead grunted as he cocked back his left arm.

The Cherokee twisted out of the way of the left hook, sending his long hair and beads into a flurry around his face. With blood dripping down the side of his mouth, he said, "Is that so? Let's find out."

Hearing that, two more Indians stepped out from the crowd and headed toward the redhead. One of them had a knife gripped in his hand and the other was reaching for a pistol kept at the small of his back.

The Indian with the pistol barely got a finger on the grip before his hand was slapped away and the pistol was plucked right from its hiding spot. Letting out an angry snarl, the man wheeled around to see who'd dared to lay a hand on him.

"Three on one just isn't sporting," Clint said as he met the other man's glare.

The Indian stood at least four inches taller than Clint

and had the build of a brick wall. Ignoring the fact that Clint had one pistol in hand and another strapped to his side, the Indian ran forward with both arms outstretched.

Clint didn't have more than a second to react before he was trampled under the Indian's feet. Rather than try to get away from the rampaging man, Clint planted his feet and sent the butt of the Indian's gun directly into its owner's gut.

The chopping blow landed on target, but bounced off the Indian's stomach like a pebble that had been tossed at a mountain. Ignoring the impact, the Indian reached out with one hand to grab hold of Clint's face. He held his other hand over his head like a blacksmith getting ready to drop his hammer upon his anvil.

Since Clint wasn't about to wait for that hammer to fall, he delivered a few strikes of his own. The first was a quick kick to the Indian's knee, which he knew landed the moment his heel cracked against the other man's trunklike leg. The next was a sharp, upward jab aimed at the Indian's elbow.

Still wobbling from Clint's kick, the Indian let out a pained grunt when his arm was suddenly snapped in the wrong direction. While none of his bones broke, they came close enough for him to let go of Clint as if he'd sprouted thorns.

By this time, the Indian with the knife had already made it over to the redhead. He didn't have much of anything to swing at since both men who'd started the tussle were now wrestling on the floor.

The redhead was forced onto his stomach by the Cherokee, just as he was stretching out with both hands toward another pistol that was lying just out of reach. Taking a handful of red hair, the Cherokee grinned and slammed the other man's face into the floorboards.

"Lift him up," the Indian with the knife said.

Once the Cherokee had turned to see where the request had come from, he was more than happy to oblige. The redhead's face almost had to be peeled up from the floor due to all the blood coming from his broken nose. His eyes blinked in a daze as he was forced to look up at the barrel of the second Indian's gun.

Before the gun's hammer was thumbed back, the Indian holding it jerked to one side and dropped to one knee. Behind him, Clint held the pistol he'd taken earlier from the other Indian like a club. His hand was wrapped around the barrel and a bit of fresh blood dripped from the handle. With a quick motion, he flipped the gun around to hold it properly.

"Even if you do have some more friends waiting to lend a hand," Clint said to the Cherokee as he sighted down the barrel, "I'd say this tips the odds against you."

The redhead was trying to say something, but the noises he made were muffled by the floor since the Cherokee had once again planted his face against the boards. Slowly, the Cherokee released his grip and raised his hands.

"Are you going to kill me?" the Cherokee asked.

"Do it," grumbled the redhead.

"Shut up," Clint snapped. "I'm not quite through saving your neck here."

"But—"

"I said shut your mouth." Shifting his attention to the Cherokee, Clint lowered the pistol. He could hear the other natives getting to their feet, and shifted so he could see if they decided to charge at him one more time. "Are you willing to let whatever this was drop?"

The Cherokee nodded.

"What about your friends there?" Clint asked.

The Cherokee's eyes narrowed as he took a look at the other two Clint was talking about. "I don't know them."

"Really? Then why'd they come running into this fight?"

"Probably because this white man has a big mouth."

Clint looked over at the redhead and stared him down in a matter of seconds.

"Did you say something stupid, Mason?" Clint asked.

Eventually, the redhead shrugged. "All I did was say that—"

Clint cut him off with a swiftly raised hand. "On second thought, I think I'll just take this gentleman's word for it. How about he buys you a drink?" he said to the Cherokee.

The Cherokee looked down at the redhead's broken nose and nodded. "Tell him to keep his mouth shut or something else will get broken next time."

"Sounds fair," Clint said before Mason could add his two cents' worth. "I'll leave this gun with the bartender. Come on, Mason. You've got some drinks to buy."

"But I ain't—"

"Just shut your mouth and buy the drinks."

NINE

A few minutes later, Clint had dropped off the pistol and delivered a bottle of whiskey to a table now occupied by the Cherokee and his two new friends. Making his way back to a table that was in another part of the room, Clint set down one beer in front of Mason and kept another for himself.

"That was some damn expensive whiskey," Mason grumbled. "They's just injuns. We could've settled this over some of the cheap stuff. They don't know no better."

Clint rolled his eyes and sipped his beer. "Why is it that every time I meet up with you, there's always fists being thrown?"

Mason smirked, but winced as he felt a stab of pain from his broken nose. Blood caked his nostrils and upper lip, but he didn't seem concerned enough to wipe it away. Instead, he merely pinched at his nose and then gave it a vicious twist.

Even with all the noise in the Holdout, Clint could still hear the crunch.

"I was the one to get my nose broke," Mason said. "I don't see anyone buying me a drink."

Clint's only response to that was a steady glare that fixed right on Mason's face and didn't waver until the other man cracked.

"All right, fine," Mason blurted out. "Maybe things do tend to get wild when I'm around. Some might see that as my special charm."

"And some might see it as a pain in the ass."

Slowly, Mason grinned. The smile caused a fresh trickle of blood from his nose, but he didn't seem to notice. "You got me there. So how the hell have you been, Clint?"

"I was doing pretty well at a card table a few days' ride from here. Then I got your message."

"I'm surprised you even got that message. I sent it off and got no reply. Hell, I even sent a telegram to Cheyenne to have someone ask around about you, and still came up empty."

"That's because Cheyenne was a bust. Too many crooked card games and men looking to pick a fight for no reason."

"Yeah," Mason grunted. "That's what I thought the last time I passed through there."

"I did get word that you were looking for me, though."

Mason perked up a bit when he heard that. "Really? From who?"

"Some men that you owe money to in Big Whiskey," Clint replied. "The only reason they tracked me down was because they figured I could make good on what you owe."

Oddly enough, Mason winced more at that than when he was forcing his nose back into line. "I didn't expect you to pay my debts, Clint. That ain't why I sent that message."

"Tell me why then. I've ridden a long way to hear this."

"You want me to get to the point? All right then." Pausing just long enough to give his nose another noisy adjustment, Mason drained half his drink and wiped his mouth with the back of his sleeve. "That injun you tussled with is a wanted man."

Clint glanced over at where Mason was pointing and shrugged. "You're a bounty hunter. You deal with plenty of wanted men. Your message said this was something bigger."

"It is. That wanted man is a killer of the worst sort. Women, children, it don't much matter." Mason pointed over at the table where the Cherokee as well as the others involved in the fight were now sharing drinks.

"He doesn't look like your typical renegade Indian," Clint said.

"That's because he ain't. He's got some others working for him and they's anything from other injuns to Mexicans and a few whites. He's even got a Chinese fella working for him to mix up some sort of concoction that he uses in his raids."

"What about the others?" Clint asked. "Are any more of the men at that table involved in what you're talking about?"

"The one I was fighting with sure is. But he ain't as high up on the ladder as the others. Far as I can tell, he's just a scout who sometimes lends a hand when the fighting gets real bad."

"What kind of fighting are we talking about here?"

Mason leaned forward and lowered his voice to a snarling whisper. "You hear about them families that were killed outside of Cheyenne a few months back?"

Clint nodded.

"And them stagecoaches that were robbed? The ones where everyone was killed, gutted, and left to rot right in the road?"

Clint's nod was slower this time. The newspapers had latched onto that story recently in a way that made the reporters seem every bit as bad as the vultures that picked those carcasses clean. "Yeah. I've heard about those."

"Them are just a few of the ones I'm talking about.

There are a few injuns leading these raids and they kill for the sport of it. But there are more folks in them raids that just are never heard from again."

"These men are slavers?"

Mason nodded grimly. "The worst kind. They take the women to sell as whores and the children to sell as God only knows what. All I know is that there are too many of them for me to handle alone."

"How do you know all this?"

"I tracked them all the way back to their camp. It's like a goddamn fort and it can move at the drop of a hat. They're ready for a posse or even a cavalry unit, but I bet a smaller group could get in and kick up some real dust."

"Good things never happen when you say something like that."

Mason grinned again, but made no move to refute what Clint had said. "I came to this saloon because these assholes have been coming in here real regular."

"And what made you decide to start a fistfight with the man you've been tracking?"

"I wanted to make sure they didn't know who I was."

Once more, Clint fixed a stern glare on Mason that caused the bounty hunter to squirm in a matter of seconds.

"Well, maybe I didn't intend on things going this far," Mason added. "But it did tell me that they got no idea I've been following them. They didn't even recognize me!"

"That's real good, Mason. Too bad your days of being nobody to them have just come to an end."

"The next time we cross paths with them, it won't matter if they recognize us or not. I seen how they operate and how they move. I can get us in close enough to free who they got and—"

"Free who?" Clint asked.

"They been collecting a fresh batch of prisoners and they aim to herd them somewhere, probably south of the border, like a bunch of cattle. If you didn't show up soon, I was gonna go in on my own before it was too late. Once they get moving, they tend to put their guard up a whole lot more."

Clint thought about all of this as he drank his beer. He could feel Mason studying him intently the entire time.

"Nearly every one of them assholes has a price on their head," Mason said. "More than enough for me to pay all my debts and be a rich man afterward. Of course, that's still considering me splitting the money with you. That's a whole lot of profit, Clint. Think about it."

"I am thinking about it." Clint set his beer down and looked over at the natives at the far table. It wasn't easy to see them from where he was sitting, but he could just make out the backs of two heads. Now that he'd watched them for a little while, they did seem to be awfully friendly for men that were supposed to have just met.

Then again, as good as Mason Barnes's intentions might be, his were usually the ones that paved the proverbial road to hell.

"You know plenty of other people, Mason. Plenty of other bounty hunters, trackers, and other folks who are in this line of work."

"True," Mason said with a nod. "But they're not too concerned with picking their targets and there's upwards of two or three dozen prisoners in that camp. Innocent folks could get killed."

"That's awfully upstanding of you," Clint said sarcastically.

"Plus, this could be the biggest job I've ever had. You know, money-wise. To be honest, no matter how long I've known most of my other associates, they're not the types to just let me walk away with my share after that mountain of cash has been split up. Besides being trustworthy, you're good enough with a gun to be of some use."

"If this is as bad as you say, I wouldn't mind looking into it."

"So you're in?"

"Not yet," Clint said. "First, I want you to show me this camp. I'm not about to hunt down anyone until I know for certain they deserve to be hunted."

Mason was already getting up. "You want to head out now or finish our beers?"

TEN

They didn't ride until a few hours before dawn. Clint and Mason met outside the town and immediately headed northwest. The path they took wasn't even much of a trail. Instead, it was a series of winding footpaths crossing over ground that was more or less flat.

The terrain opened up a bit before too long. After breaking out of a thick bunch of woods, they joined up with a more common trail used by stagecoaches and traders. That path branched off again, leading them into a wide expanse of grasslands with the mountains visible in the distance. With the moonlight washing over the swaying field, it looked more like an ocean than land.

"You trying to get me lost?" Clint asked after Mason finally pulled back on his reins.

"Here I thought you couldn't get lost, Clint."

"I asked if you were trying. I never said it was working."

"Bullshit. I almost get lost every time I come out this way."

"So where's this camp you were talking about?"

"Right over there," Mason replied while extending his hand to point to the north.

Clint looked in that direction to find what appeared to be a small wagon train. After squinting at it for a little longer, he picked out more wagons gathered nearby and yet another group near the second one. Each group was circled, as any overly cautious expedition was likely to do in open territory.

"See those wagons?" Mason asked. "That's the camp."

"They're not exactly hiding from anyone."

"No, but they've got riders patrolling the perimeter and scouts posted on every bit of high ground. That's why we had to ride through bramble country just to get close enough to get a peek."

"You don't think we were spotted?"

Mason shook his head. "I know we weren't spotted. They ain't the types to quietly shoo away unwanted guests."

"Then how did you get close enough to see anything for yourself?"

"I worked my way in on foot. Took me three days of creeping and waiting, but I got in. Even so, it was hairy getting back out."

"I don't have enough supplies for three days."

"And you won't need 'em," Mason replied. "You wanted proof these are bad men? I'm about to give it to you. Just be ready to take advantage of the opening when you get it."

Clint had an idea what Mason might be planning. Before he could say a word to talk him out of it, the bounty hunter was already riding away. After putting about twenty yards between himself and Clint, Mason snapped his reins.

His spotted mustang trotted for a ways without making much noise. The horse was lighter on its feet than its rider, which allowed it to get another thirty paces before it was in danger of being spotted. Then, Mason dug his heels into the mustang's side and snapped the reins again. That caused the horse to break into a full gallop, which sounded like rolling thunder in the otherwise quiet night.

"Jesus Christ," Clint muttered to himself. "It's a wonder that man hasn't gotten himself killed by now."

Whatever Clint might have thought about Mason's methods, he couldn't argue with the results. Not only had he gotten several members of the patrol and lookouts to show themselves, but he'd even gotten a bunch of them to follow him away from their posts. After a group of men got on their horses and took off after Mason, they left behind a hole that Clint could have driven his own wagon through.

"All right then," Clint said while snapping Eclipse's reins. "Let's see what we can see."

Hunkering down low over Eclipse's back, Clint got the Darley Arabian moving at about half speed. That way, they covered a good amount of ground without making too much noise. Then again, Clint could have made all the noise he wanted and still wouldn't have been able to compete with the ruckus Mason had stirred up.

Already, he'd started yelling like a crazy man. His mustang was whinnying and stomping its hooves like it had been possessed. While Clint might not have been able to make out the exact words that the other men were shouting at Mason, he could definitely tell they weren't kind.

Shaking his head, but also laughing at the same time, Clint hopped from the saddle, slapped Eclipse's rump, and started running toward the camp.

ELEVEN

Eclipse galloped off toward the same trees that Clint and Mason had used for cover. Clint had no doubt the Darley Arabian wouldn't wander off too far to be called back later. The stallion had been through too much with Clint to just leave him without seeking him out again soon after. If Clint had his way, the horse wouldn't have to wait long at all.

Already, Clint could tell that Mason hadn't been stretching the truth where the camp's security was concerned. On his way toward the closest group of wagons, Clint spotted several armed men. Most of those men were trying to get a look at the commotion in the distance, which allowed Clint to sneak right past them.

The first few guards were easy. After that, things got a lot trickier.

A campfire was lit in the middle of each group of circled wagons. There were the normal sights and smells accompanying the fire, including people talking, pots clanking, and food cooking. Outside the fire's glow, however, was another group of men dressed in dark clothes and standing in the shadows with pistols on their hips and rifles in their hands. There were even a few dogs tied to the wheel of a wagon.

Clint steered clear of the dogs and slowly crept his way past the guards. If not for the continued distraction Mason was providing, he doubted he'd ever be able to get half as close.

Suddenly, a twig snapped and a boot crunched into the ground no more than five feet from where Clint was hiding.

"What the hell's going on?" a gruff voice asked.

There was another step, followed by a different voice. "Some drunk's out for a ride by the looks of it."

More of the heavier steps thumped against the dirt. Clint kept his belly just above the ground and scurried under the closest wagon he could find. Even before he'd pulled his boots under the wagon, the source of those heavy steps came into view.

It was a large man with a round belly hanging over his belt. A long mustache hung past his chin and a gold tooth glinted with reflected firelight. "That him out there?" he asked.

The man he was speaking to was out of Clint's sight. Even so, the sound of his voice and footsteps meant he had to be smaller than the man with the potbelly. "That's the one."

From where he was, Clint could only see the bigger man's face for a few seconds. After that, he could only make out one pair of boots standing beside another pair.

"What the hell's he doing?" the gruffer voice asked.

"Riding around like a damn fool."

"Someone better've gone out to shut his mouth."

"Oh, there's plenty out there to shut him up. If'n he don't play his cards right, that drunk might not make it home tonight."

There was a silence between the two men. Clint shifted

forward slightly, but stopped when he heard the crunch of gravel scraping beneath him. Stretching his neck out as much as he could, he tried to get a look at either man.

The one with the potbelly walked forward enough for Clint to see most of him. He was a big man, but most of his girth was around his waist. Long, stringy hair came down from the back of an old hat. One of his boots jangled with a rusty spur.

With a quickness that took Clint by surprise, the big man spun around. Although Clint wanted to crawl back under the wagon, he pulled his head in and stayed still. If the shadows weren't thick enough to cover him, a few more inches wouldn't help him much anyway.

"How close did he get to us?" the big man asked.

"Eh . . . I don't know."

"You better fucking know," the big man snarled as he reached out to grab hold of the other one. "I don't pay this many men to keep watch just so a drunk can ride up and see what's going on in here."

"He didn't get close! I swear it!"

"How close?"

"No closer than he is right now. Jesus, Umberto, it's just some drunk out for a ride."

After watching the display Mason was putting on for a few more seconds, Umberto let the smaller man go. "He didn't get any closer than that? Now's the time to change your story if it needs changing."

"On my mother's grave, he got no closer than that."

"All right then. Just make sure someone shuts him up quick. That ruckus is giving me a headache."

With that, the heavy footsteps thumped toward Clint. By this time, Clint had managed to scoot a bit farther under the wagon and was staring out from the shadows as Umberto stomped toward him. He could feel every one of the big man's steps as they pounded against the dirt. Before those steps stopped rattling through Clint's bones, the smaller man had already run off to climb onto the back of the nearest horse.

When Clint let out his breath, he realized he'd been holding it for close to a minute.

TWELVE

Clint crawled out from under the wagon and got to his feet. Now that Umberto and the smaller man were gone, that left an even bigger hole in the camp's defenses. In reality, that only meant two or three of the individual wagons were in Clint's grasp.

The first wagon Clint inspected was the one he'd been hiding under. It was a simple covered wagon like those used by any number of folks headed to California during any of the great westward rushes. In fact, it looked as if that very wagon could have crossed the country at least three times. Its wheels were new, but the rest of it was chipped, cracked, and warped from being in too many rainstorms.

A stained tarp covered the top and was tied shut for the night. After making certain nobody was watching, Clint snuck up and pulled open the tarp just enough for him to get a look inside. All he saw was black. Still, there was something vaguely familiar about the bulky shape he saw closest to the gate.

The smell of gun oil and powder, on the other hand, was unmistakable.

"Good Lord," Clint whispered. The words came out before he had a chance to stop them. Fortunately, there wasn't anyone close enough to hear them.

After taking a quick look around, Clint figured he had at least another thirty seconds or so before he needed to move on. There were a few men closer to the fire, but they were facing another direction and walking away from Clint's wagon.

Clint reached into the wagon and took hold of one of the several stacks of crates inside. He pulled himself in and barely managed to find a place to set his feet before tumbling out again. The wagon was so filled with crates and other materials that Clint had to get himself positioned in an uncomfortable tangle of arms and legs just to stay inside the wagon.

The crates weren't nailed shut, so Clint was able to take a look inside. Almost all that he opened were packed with rifles, pistols, and plenty of bullets for each. There were also a few boxes of dynamite, but that wasn't what interested him the most.

What captured the majority of his attention was the large piece of equipment in the rear of the wagon. Propped up on a set of crates and covered with a greasy tarp, there was a Gatling gun complete with several crates of ammunition. When he got behind the gun, he discovered a crude seat made out of more stacked boxes.

As much as Clint would have liked to take inventory of the weapons in that wagon, he could already hear the commotion outside starting to die down. He took a peek out of the wagon, saw the coast was clear, and then hopped down.

By now, he was plenty used to crawling from one dark spot to another and was able to examine two more wagons.

One of them was packed with clothes, supplies, and some more dynamite. The other was carrying a much different sort of cargo.

Clint peeled back the tarp at the back of that third wagon and reflexively went for his gun when he saw several pairs of eyes staring back at him. Before he cleared leather, his eyes were able to pick out the details of a few faces.

Some of them were no more than five years old.

Some were girls in their teens or twenties.

Every one of them was petrified.

Lifting a finger to his lips, Clint motioned for them to be quiet as he climbed into the wagon. Despite the fact that they were packed in tighter than the guns in the other wagons, they still managed to scoot away from him before Clint closed the tarp behind him.

"How many of you are in here?" he whispered.

Nobody said a word.

"I'm not going to hurt anyone. I just need to know how many of you there are."

With his eyes adjusting to the thick shadows inside the wagon, Clint could make out more and more of the frightened faces staring back at him. There were more in there than he'd originally thought and the longer he looked, the more he saw piled up on top of each other.

"There's thirteen," came a trembling voice.

Clint searched for who'd spoken and found a little boy glaring up defiantly at him from where he was huddled on the floor.

"Thirteen of you?" Clint asked.

The boy nodded. "Used to be fourteen."

"What happened to the other one?"

"She left."

"Where did she go?"

As he talked to the boy, Clint could sense the tension inside the wagon fading away. It was like a fog that melted off after enough sun had shone through.

"She left a little while ago," the boy continued.

"She left on her own, or was she taken away?"

"She left."

"Do you know how long ago?"

The boy shook his head. "Is it daytime outside?"

Before he could answer, Clint could feel someone tugging at his sleeve. It was one of the young women. She was a slender girl with a pale face and wide eyes. By the looks of her, she was in her early teens.

"You're not one of them," she whispered.

"No, I'm not."

"Then you've got to help us. Please!"

As she raised her voice, Clint reached out to quickly and gently place his hand upon her lips. Seeing her flinch away from him didn't set right with Clint, but it was better than drawing a whole mess of armed killers to the wagon.

"You've got to keep your voice down," Clint whispered.

"You've got to get us out of here, mister. They're going to take us away and sell us."

"Are any of you hurt?"

"Just bumps and bruises. But once we're in Canada, Lord only knows what will happen."

"You're going to Canada?"

"They're taking us there. At least, that's what they tell us."

"They got no reason to lie," one of the others said. "After all the men they killed when they took us, they know we can't go nowhere."

"Nobody's gotten away before," added the little boy. "Not until tonight."

The woman who'd spoken first leaned in close to whisper in Clint's ear. "She didn't get away. One of them came for her. You've got to get us out of here. Please."

"When do you think you'll be leaving for Canada?" Clint asked.

"It's going to be soon. I can feel it."

"If I could get all of you out of here safely, I would. What I need you to do is sit tight and wait for me to come back."

"No!" the girl said as her eyes grew wide and her face turned pale. "We can't stay here any longer. You've got to help us."

Clint took hold of her by the shoulders and looked directly into her eyes. "I've only got one gun and a few extra bullets. That won't do any good against the firepower these men have. I need to get out of here so I can come back with a plan and the means to carry it out. Do you understand?"

She stared at him blankly while all the other captives started to whimper.

"All of you need to trust in me," Clint said. "Trust that I'll come back. If I try to get any of you out right now, it'll only put you in danger. If these men wanted to kill you, you'd already be dead."

He knew that was going to upset them, but he was quick to go on even though he heard some muted sobbing.

"That means you'll be safe until I get back," Clint assured them. "I know for a fact they need you all alive, so if you keep quiet and cooperate as best you can, you'll be just fine until I can get you out of here. And I will get you out of here. I promise that."

The sobbing had stopped and now every eye was focused upon Clint.

"I'm leaving now, but I'll be back," he told them. "I need you all to be brave and be strong so you can be ready when I do."

There were nods coming from everyone in the wagon.

"Most importantly, I need you to promise you won't tell anyone I was here." Looking over at the little boy, Clint added, "When I come back for you, I want it to be a surprise for the men shoving you around."

"Yer damn right it'll be a surprise," the kid said.

Clint snuck out of the wagon and made his way back to the trees outside camp. Eclipse was waiting for him.

THIRTEEN

When Clint met up with Mason again, he found the bounty hunter perched on his horse like a general who'd just conquered an entire country. The man's rough features were contorted into a self-satisfied grin, which only grew brighter as Clint got closer.

"Now that was a piece of work," Mason said. "We're almost a mile away and I can still hear them talking about me."

"Oh, they were talking all right," Clint said. "That's how I was able to get out of there even after you'd been driven away."

"You spent a little more time in there than I expected. I was just about to start planning how to bust you out."

Clint reached out to pat Mason's shoulder. "You did a hell of a job acting like a crazy drunk, but let's not get too full of yourself."

"Did you see what you needed to see?"

"And then some. I only got to get a look at a fraction of that camp and I already know they've got more firepower than most forts."

"See? I told ya."

"You were definitely right," Clint admitted. "They're loaded for bear and could probably hold back an attack from two or three posses at once. Even if the law did manage to get through, it wouldn't be till after a hell of a lot of men were gunned down."

Mason nodded the entire time as he rode alongside Clint. When the bounty hunter steered away from the path they'd taken to get to the camp, Clint followed him.

"I found the prisoners as well," Clint continued. "Thirteen of them all packed into a single wagon. Actually, it used to be fourteen according to them."

"You talked to the prisoners?" Mason asked.

"For a little bit. It broke my heart to leave them there, but I didn't have much choice."

"Thank God. If we're to do anything against those assholes, I'll need your help to do it. So what do you say? Are we going through with this?"

"You're damn right we are."

Mason smiled and pumped his fist in the air. "Hot damn! That's what I wanted to hear."

"But only on one condition," Clint said as he brought Eclipse to a sudden stop.

Mason pulled back on his reins. "What condition?"

"That you go in there wanting to rescue those prisoners as much as you want to drag in those killers."

"Of course! What kind of . . ." Mason was stopped by the intense glare coming from Clint. "All right. You have my word. I'll put both of those things at the top of my list."

"Good."

"But we're not going back in after them prisoners tonight," Mason added. "I feel for them folks too, but I ain't prepared to go in with guns blazing this second."

Clint nodded. "I agree. If those men are asking for a ransom or planning on selling their prisoners off, they need to keep them healthy."

"There ain't been any ransom demands as far as I know and believe me, I've checked. Near as I can tell, the families of them prisoners figure those that are missing are dead and buried."

"As odd as it may sound, that works in our favor," Clint said. "Those prisoners were under control and the guards were already being drawn in while you were still out for your ride. I was able to slip in and out, but there's no way all of them could make a move like that without alerting the whole camp."

"My sentiments exactly. So are we in on this together?" Mason asked while extending his hand over to Clint.

Clint shook the bounty hunter's hand. "We're in."

Hearing that, Mason snapped his reins and launched his mustang into a gallop.

Not only did Clint notice that Mason was headed in a different direction than the way they'd approached the camp, but he also noticed that he'd already been led to a different spot while they'd been talking. "Where are you going?" he asked as he steered Eclipse toward Mason's back.

In no time at all, the Darley Arabian caught up to the mustang. Riding alongside the smaller horse, Clint asked, "Where are you going?"

"I got a little surprise for you."

Before Clint had a chance to ask another question, Mason had led him into another group of trees. This was a small cluster consisting mostly of bushes, but was thick enough to hide one slender young woman.

"Who's that?" Clint asked when he caught sight of her.

"That," Mason said, "is your fourteenth prisoner."

FOURTEEN

Clint swung down from the saddle before Eclipse had even come to a stop. He hit the ground running and didn't slow down until he was close enough to see the frightened look on that woman's face.

She was a bit older than what he might have guessed on first sight. That was a common impression he got from most Indian women. Even in the pale light of the moon, her dark complexion was plain to see. Her hair was like thick, watery shadows running along either side of her face, and was tied into two braids that hung down past her shoulders.

"Don't be afraid," Clint said as he got closer. "I'm not going to hurt you."

The woman looked past Clint to Mason. Once she saw the bounty hunter nod his approval, she ventured out to meet Clint halfway.

"I found her on my way back from that camp," Mason explained. "Damn near trampled her is more like it."

All it took was an outstretched hand on Clint's part to get the young woman the rest of the way out of her hiding place. Once she was out, she practically ran into Clint's arms.

The woman was dressed in a skirt made out of animal skins that were tanned to become softer than most fabrics. It was decorated with a few simple designs along with the occasional bead or two hanging from a stubborn fringe. Her blouse was similar to what plenty of other women wore, but seemed somewhat exotic on her. Perhaps it was the way her coffee-colored skin and toned curves contrasted with the loose white cloth.

Or perhaps it was the natural beauty in her brown eyes and strong features.

"It's all right," Clint said as he held the trembling woman. "We're not going to hurt you. Nobody is."

"When are we leaving this place?" she asked.

"How's right now sound?"

She nodded vigorously, and then stepped back as if she'd only just realized she was hugging a complete stranger.

"Do you have a name?" Clint asked.

"My name among my people is . . . well . . . it means Willow in your language."

"That's a pretty name. Let's get out of here, Willow, so you can tell us what happened before we crossed paths."

Clint climbed onto Eclipse's back and held out a hand for Willow. She didn't turn her nose up at his offer, but she just simply didn't need it. With as much trouble as anyone else might go through to climb a single step, she jumped onto the saddle behind Clint.

"You might want to hold on," Clint said. "We'll be riding pretty fast."

"Ride as fast as you can," she replied without placing one arm around Clint.

"Suit yourself." With that, Clint flicked the reins and got the Darley Arabian moving at a quick walk. Not only did Willow stay perfectly in place behind him, but he barely even knew she was there. He looked over at Mason and saw the bounty hunter nodding in admiration.

Both horses took off running and put the slavers' camp well behind them.

The ride back went smoothly. Once they'd gotten far enough away for Clint and Mason to stop checking to see if they were being followed, they rode into town and headed straight for the hotel where Mason was staying. Rather than rent a second room, Clint snuck Willow in through the back of the hotel and took her to the room they already had.

Willow sat on a chair in a corner, which allowed her to see the door, window, and everything else in the room. Her eyes fluttered shut and her head drooped forward.

Stepping toward Willow, Mason whispered, "Should I wake her up?"

When he was within arm's reach of her, he saw Willow's eyes snap open as she pressed herself further into the corner.

"We have some questions we need to ask," he said.

Clint stepped in and moved Mason back. "It can wait until we've rested up."

The bounty hunter shrugged and walked over to his bed. His back hit the threadbare mattress and he let out a noisy, prolonged sigh.

Apart from a broken dresser and cracked washbasin, there was only a stool left inside the room. Clint placed that stool between the bed and Willow's corner before sitting down and leaning against a wall.

That made Willow comfortable enough to close her eyes again and keep them shut.

FIFTEEN

After some much-needed rest, Mason turned in his hotel key while Clint and Willow slipped out the back. They met up a few streets away and rode out of town. It wasn't until they were out of sight of the place that Willow finally started to breathe at a regular pace again.

"Where are we going?" she asked.

"We had a deal," Clint replied. "Remember?"

"Yes. That's right."

"Tell me about what happened in that camp."

"Those men came into my village and burned it to the ground. Some got away, but the ones who fought were killed like animals. Those men gathered up all the women and children they could find and threw us into wagons."

"I saw the other prisoners," Clint told her. "They looked like they were in good health."

Willow was on the back of Clint's horse, so he couldn't see the way she lowered her eyes. He didn't have to see her in order to sense the sadness in her voice when she said, "The men wanted to make sure we looked good when we were sold. They told us that they would only keep the ones that would get the best price. We could either behave or die. There was nothing in between."

"So they didn't hurt you?" Mason asked.

After a long pause, Willow said, "They didn't want to mark us. One of the men who gave orders to the rest . . . he said to keep the women so they could please whoever brought us."

Mason furrowed his brow. "Huh? Oh, I see."

"Where were they taking you?" Clint asked.

"North. Into the snowy country."

"Canada?"

"Yes. They were waiting to gather enough men so they could sell all of us at one time. Then they could start over and steal more people from their families and make more money."

"How long till this happens?" Mason asked.

"I think they were going to leave in a day or so. That is what my brother told me."

Clint glanced over his shoulder to get a look at her. "Your brother? Is he one of the prisoners?"

She shook her head slowly. "He left our village years ago. I thought I would never see him again, but when I was captured I saw him among the men who raided my village."

Mason let out a whistle and shook his head. "Raided his own village, huh? That's cold-blooded."

If looks could kill, the glare Willow shot at the bounty hunter would have been enough to send Mason and his horse to their graves a few times over. "Ka'lanu would never hurt his own people. He was among the men who raided my village, but he knew nothing about that until he found me."

"What happened, Willow?" Clint asked in a soothing tone to draw her attention away from Mason before she lunged at him.

Willow's hands settled on her knees as she turned to

look away from both men. Her body adjusted to every one of Eclipse's steps as if doing so was the most natural thing in the world. "After I was captured, I didn't see the sky for days. We were let out only once every night and on one of those nights, I saw my brother at the other side of the camp.

"He saw me too, but didn't come to talk to me right away. When he did come, I thought it was a dream. When I told him about what happened, he said it was a nightmare."

"Didn't he know what was going on?" Clint asked.

She shook her head. "No. He would never ride with such men if he knew what they were. They lied to him. That is why he set me free."

"One of the prisoners said you'd been taken off by someone," Clint recalled. "I guess that explains that."

"My brother let me out, but could not go with me."

"Did he tell you anything about what route them wagons would take?" Mason asked. "Or about how many guns they got? Or anything we could use?"

"All I know is what I saw," Willow answered. "When they raided my village, they burned it to the ground. The air was filled with gunshots and the dirt was wet with blood."

"That's a real help," Mason grumbled.

Clint shot the bounty hunter a look that was more than enough to silence him. By the time he turned to Willow, that look had been replaced with a comforting smile. "Are you certain there wasn't anything you might have heard? Did they mention a town or any specific place they might be headed?"

Willow closed her eyes and took a moment to think. Suddenly, her eyes snapped open and she said, "Atsina!"

"Gesundheit," Mason said with a laugh. "What the hell is asteema supposed to mean?"

"Atsina," Clint corrected. "They're a tribe in northeast Montana."

Willow nodded and focused her attention solely upon Clint. "I didn't hear much, but I heard one of the men tell the others that they would need to be on the lookout for Atsina."

"That's a big help to us, Willow. Thank you." Turning to Mason, Clint said, "This gives us a point where we know those wagons will be going."

"Will they be looking for them Atsina to help them or to get in their way?"

"I've run into a few of them, but I couldn't answer that question for certain. For now, all we know is where we're headed." Clint brought Eclipse to a stop, which immediately caused Willow to tense up behind him. Although they'd been on the move for a bit, they hadn't put more than a mile or so between themselves and the camp.

"I need to talk to your brother," Clint said as he turned to look at Willow. "Is there any way you could arrange that?"

She paused and lowered her head. After some deliberation, she looked back up to meet Clint's eyes. "I can send a signal to him. He told me to do so if I got in trouble before I got far away from the camp. But I will only tell you if you are the only one to use it. Not him," she added while nodding at Mason.

"Fine. We can only afford to have one of us at the meet anyhow."

"Great," Mason grumbled. "I see how I rank in this."

Ignoring the bounty hunter's complaints, Clint said to Willow, "You can send the signal yourself and can come along to pay him a visit. Mason, I need you to keep an eye on those wagons and make sure they don't get away from us."

Mason let out a choppy laugh. "They're the size of three wagon trains, Clint. I don't think they'll get away from us."

"They know how to slip past the law and the military, so I'm sure they've got enough tricks to slip by us if we're not careful."

Reluctantly, Mason nodded. "I see your point."

"Willow, what's this signal you mentioned?"

Clint barely felt a brush of movement behind him before he heard the soft impact of her feet against the ground. Willow made her way to some bushes to gather up some branches and other materials before heading to a nearby tree. "I need a knife," she said.

Clint tossed her his pocketknife.

She caught it and immediately started carving out a hunk of wood. After she had what she needed, she returned to Eclipse's side and hopped onto the stallion's back. Without a word, she began carving the wood.

SIXTEEN

The wagons were moving at a steady pace, rolling in three groups headed north. To all appearances, they were just a large group of travelers striking out for any of the numerous reasons that folks would have for leaving the comfort of wherever they'd been. To those that knew even less about them, the wagons might just look like two or three separate expeditions sharing company for this particular stretch of road.

Clint had skirted around them all day long. It had been a real chore keeping an eye out for scouts and staying out of sight while also keeping tabs on the larger group. Thankfully, the wagons made enough noise for Clint or Willow to hear them most of the time even though the slavers couldn't be seen.

The trail had led between a series of rolling hills, allowing Clint to gain some high ground. Sometimes, that made his task a lot easier. Other times, it made it more possible for the scouts to catch sight of him. Clint had counted at least four scouts riding ahead and to the sides of the larger group of wagons. They rode in something of a pattern as they circled the group and took turns running ahead to get a look at the trail before the wagons got to it.

Clint crested a rise and thought he'd been spotted when he saw the rider on top of another rise looking straight at him. He soon got a wave from that rider, showing him that it was actually Mason. Clint returned the wave and then pointed off to the west.

Glancing off in that direction, Mason nodded, waved again, and snapped his reins. He took off at a gallop that was just loud enough to catch some attention. When a few of the scouts rode to investigate, Clint glanced back at Willow.

"All right," he said. "Now's about the time for that signal of yours."

She nodded and took hold of the piece of wood she'd been carving. In the few hours that they'd been riding, she'd managed to hollow out three small openings through the middle of her piece of wood. Two openings were holes that she used to thread through some of the weeds she'd plucked from the ground, and the other was larger and shaped with a lip on one end.

The weeds that were tied to the wood were also wrapped around a few small rocks, which added to the wood's weight. That way, when she held onto the other end of the weeds and spun the wood over her head, it made a high-pitched whistle.

Clint winced at the sound of it, mainly because it was even more piercing than he'd anticipated. Once Willow got the contraption spinning at the right pace, however, the whistle evened out into something that sounded more like a dying bird than anything man-made.

"There he is," Willow said hopefully.

Sure enough, one of the scouts had stopped and turned to look directly at the source of the whistle. He steered his horse toward Clint and ran straight for him.

"You're sure that's your brother?" Clint asked uneasily.

"That's him. I know it."

"All right then." Clint pulled on the reins and brought Eclipse around. One last look toward the wagons showed that there was still only one scout headed his way. Riding down the other side of the hill, Clint kept his hand near his gun and hoped for the best.

They didn't have to wait long before the sound of hooves against the dirt filled their ears. Even before Clint got much of a look at the scout's face, Willow was hopping from the saddle and running toward the approaching horse.

"Ka'lanu!" she said with her arms outstretched.

The scout's face was stern, but soon broke into a wide smile when he saw Willow. He brought his horse to a stop and jumped down with an ease that made Willow's grace pale in comparison.

"What are you doing here?" Ka'lanu asked.

Before Willow could answer, the big native scout had already set his sights on Clint.

"And why is he with you?" Ka'lanu asked.

Clint got down from the saddle and walked toward the pair. "I should ask you the same thing. The last time I saw you, you were tussling with a friend of mine."

Ka'lanu was dressed in a set of skins that weren't quite what he'd been wearing in the Holdout Saloon, but he still had the same bits of gold and beads threaded through his hair. The Cherokee also had the same fire in his eyes as when he'd been throwing punches at Mason.

By the look on his face, the Cherokee was none too happy to have crossed paths with Clint again.

SEVENTEEN

"Your friend has a big mouth," Ka'lanu said. "If he said those same things now, I would react the same way."

"I agree with you on that point. What I need to know is if you can put that aside to work with me."

Looking at his sister, the Cherokee got an enthusiastic nod. "Work with you on what?"

"Helping to make sure what happened to your sister doesn't happen to anyone else."

"I ride with these men. Why would I betray them?"

"Because I believe your sister when she told me you didn't know what they were truly up to. Even if you did have some idea, that must have changed when you saw what they did to your own flesh and blood."

Slowly, Ka'lanu turned his face away as if he was ashamed to look either of them in the eye. Then, after pulling in a deep breath, he forced himself to stand tall. "When I left my people, I wanted to have a better life. I soon found out that I could not do so without breaking the white man's laws. If they had their way, every man with my color would be fenced into a patch of dead land or shot.

"I met the big belly and he gave me a job and paid me as much as he paid anyone else in his group. He told me we were robbing from the railroads and from land barons. Either way, I figured I was taking back some of what had already been taken from my people." Looking into Willow's face, he added, "I was going to come back for you. I was going to hand over enough money for all of us to buy our own land. You must believe me."

"I do," Willow said as she patted her brother's cheek.

Turning to Clint, Ka'lanu said, "All I am is a scout. I ride ahead and look in on where the wagons are going. Many times, I don't even sleep with the rest of the group. I'm hardly ever this close to the rest. Only recently, the big belly started to show me more of what was going on. When I realized what was in those wagons, I knew that everything else he spoke to me was a lie."

"Who is the big belly?" Clint asked.

"He is the one who leads them all. His name is Umberto."

"I think I crossed paths with that one."

"He fights with blades more than the guns he wears and his tongue is from a snake's mouth."

"Can you tell me where the wagons are headed?"

"Into the snowy country. North into Canada."

"By what route?"

"The big belly makes those decisions and doesn't tell the scouts until the wagons are ready to go there. For now, we are heading straight north. I will be riding ahead after sunset to find the best way."

"I think I know where Umberto's leaning as far as that's concerned," Clint said. "There's a town I know outside of Atsina territory. It's called Sharps."

Ka'lanu nodded. "We have traded with the Atsina before."

"Do you think you could steer the wagons toward Sharps?"

"I can."

"Great. Now, will you be making any more stops along the way? Besides getting supplies. I mean, will Umberto be collecting any more prisoners?"

Shaking his head, Ka'lanu replied, "All four wagons are full."

"All four?" Willow asked.

"Yours was just one group of captives," Ka'lanu told his sister. "There are almost as many of them as there are guns. And if you're going to ask me to set those others free, Mr. Adams, then I cannot. The big belly will kill them all rather than lose them. When I set my sister free, I was lucky to have the spirits with me. I would not gamble that the spirits would protect them all."

"Do you think they'll be safe along the way?" Clint asked.

"As safe as they can be while still remaining prisoners. I do know that the big belly does not want them harmed before being sold. I have heard that much from some of the other men now that they think I am one of them."

"So you've been let into the main organization?"

"I suppose, but it sickens me."

"Why haven't you left?"

Ka'lanu didn't have an answer to that right away. Instead, his shame seemed to grow with each passing second.

"I'll tell you why," Clint said. "Because you want to take them apart from the inside. Isn't that why you let the other men live after freeing your sister?"

Although Ka'lanu didn't answer with any words, the look in his eye told Clint that he was on the right track.

"You seem like a good man," Clint continued. "I know if I found myself in your situation, I couldn't just turn my back on all of that and leave. I'd want to do something about it. Well, if you feel that way, I might be able to help."

Ka'lanu studied Clint's face for a few seconds before shifting his eyes to his sister. After seeing her smile at him, the Cherokee nodded slowly. "I have thought some of those things, but there are too many of them for one man to make a dent. Bravery and a strong arm is no match for rifles and gunpowder."

"A few men can make a stand against those slavers," Clint said. "No matter how many guns they have. I have an idea of how to do this, and I've got someone else to help me. Those prisoners will have a much better chance if someone like you helps from the inside of that camp."

"Those prisoners would rather die trying to escape than be herded north and sold off like cattle," Willow said. "I know that for a fact."

"You trust this white man?" Ka'lanu asked.

Willow nodded. "He has treated me well."

"And the one with the big mouth?"

"He's the one who found me after you set me free. He took me away from the camp and hid me from the others."

Nodding, Ka'lanu extended his arm toward Clint. Clint took hold of his arm just beneath the elbow as the Cherokee did the same.

"I will do as you ask. But if you put my sister in danger," Ka'lanu said, "or if I learn you are lying to me, I will skin you like a deer."

"All right then," Clint replied. "See you in Sharps."

EIGHTEEN

For the next few days, Clint and Mason weren't exactly taking Ka'lanu at his word. They didn't say as much to Willow, but they didn't allow themselves to get too far away from the wagons as they worked their way northwest. Mason made it clear to Clint that he didn't trust the Cherokee as soon as Clint told him about his conversation with Ka'lanu. Of course, considering their history, that wasn't too surprising.

As far as Clint was concerned, there was too much at stake for him to blindly trust a man he'd just met. He could see the love Willow had for her brother, so he couldn't exactly ask her how much he should trust him and expect an unbiased response. That left Clint to the one thing that he trusted implicitly: his own instincts.

To that day, his instincts had never let him down. During those next couple days of riding, he felt like those instincts were the only things guiding him from one spot to the next. Clint, Mason, and Willow were keeping pace with the wagons and staying just outside the scouts' range, making for a tricky balance between keeping up and keeping alive.

Clint and Mason rode on either side of the wagons, trading places every couple of hours. That way, they could compare notes when they crossed paths and switched sides. The pattern suited them rather well, allowing Clint and Mason to ride ahead of the wagons and scouts like a boat being pushed in front of a wave.

It was getting close to sundown when Clint drew Eclipse to a stop and waited for Mason. The bounty hunter arrived on schedule and came up alongside Eclipse.

"We're about another day's ride from that town of yours," Mason said. "But it don't look to me like those wagons have any intention of heading there."

"Ka'lanu said the scouts don't know where they're headed until Umberto tells them where to go."

"They must have their own routes set up. I doubt they'll just forget about them and head in another direction."

Clint shook his head. "They're not just some outlaw gang that can keep to their normal trails. They're a large caravan and they need to stick to the bigger roads. It makes sense that they wouldn't take the same route twice in a row. They'd have to be able to steer clear of the law or any number of things that might slow them down."

"Yeah, I guess you're right. Otherwise, they wouldn't need no scouts."

"I did see some of the scouts turn to the east," Clint pointed out. "That would take them in the direction of Sharps."

"And what if them wagons don't turn?"

"Then we come up with a new plan."

"I still don't know what you got in mind with this plan," Mason said.

Swinging down from his saddle, Clint broke off a stick and began drawing in the dirt. Soon, Willow and Mason were standing beside him.

"First of all," Clint said as he drew, "Sharps is a small town where I know a few people we can trust. It's also a place that might be of interest to a few scouts or other men from that caravan. At the very least, I figure we can get a hold of a few of Umberto's men so we can question them as to where, exactly, they intend on selling their prisoners."

Mason nodded and smiled. "So far, so good."

"Second, there's only one trail that leads out of Sharps which heads toward Canada." Clint drew a line from one spot in the dirt to a spot between two large ovals. "That trail leads between these two rock walls for a stretch of at least a quarter of a mile."

"You sure about that?" Mason asked.

"I nearly got killed escorting a payroll through there, so yeah, I'm sure." Glancing at Willow, he asked, "Do you think you could get ahold of your brother once we get to Sharps?"

"Probably."

"Good, because I'll need him to see if he can get the wagons holding the prisoners separated from the rest."

"And what if he can't?" Mason grunted.

"Then I'll figure out a way to get it done. All that's important is that we get those wagons separated while they're in this canyon. That way," Clint explained as he drew more lines on thc map, "you can ride in this way and I can ride in through here to take over those wagons and start driving them south."

"And what about them guns and all them men?"

"When those wagons come through, it won't matter how many men or guns they've got. We'll have the high ground and that should be enough to get the drop on them."

Mason studied the drawing in the dirt and let out a low whistle. "There's an awful lot riding on them wagons rolling down that stretch of road. What makes me nervous is that they ain't even pointed in that direction yet."

"If Ka'lanu does his part, they should turn east real soon. Just to be safe, though, one of us should stay with the wagons while the other goes into Sharps."

"I guess I'll be the one to stay with the wagons," Mason grumbled. "Especially since that brother of hers would probably still like to knock my head off my shoulders."

"I don't know about all that," Clint said. "But it might be better for me to be the one to go into town with Willow."

"Are we going to find the law?" Willow asked. "When my brother set me free, he told me to run to the nearest town so I could tell the law where to find the rest of the prisoners. He made me promise."

Clint was staring down at the map he'd drawn as if he could see things beyond the simple lines and circles. "Something tells me that those slavers have a plan for getting away if the law comes at them."

"Yeah," Mason said. "Like setting fire to the wagons with the prisoners in 'em and taking off with the rest."

Clint's eyes narrowed as he let out a slow breath. "Something like that."

Willow's jaw dropped and she looked back and forth between the men as if she couldn't believe what she was hearing. "Would anyone do such a thing?"

Looking over at her, Clint said, "Think back to when your village was attacked and ask yourself that same question again."

Willow's face took on a haunted quality, and she nodded slowly.

"Once we get those prisoners separated, attacking those slavers from this bottleneck is our best bet," Clint said while tapping the spot in the dirt he'd drawn.

Mason squatted down to look at it as if he was trying to see what Clint had found in his drawing earlier. Instead, he shook his head. "Sounds to me like a real good way to get ourselves killed."

"If you've got a better idea, then I'm willing to listen."

"Nah," Mason said with a grin. "I wanted you with me on this because you know how to walk through hell and come out the other side. Guess it would be foolish to question you now."

"If we do this right," Clint said as he wiped away his drawing with his boot, "hell is exactly where those slavers are headed."

NINETEEN

After arranging for a spot and time to meet up again, Clint and Mason parted ways. Clint wasn't too happy with the situation, but there wasn't much else they could do since the men they were after were splitting up as well. Willow came along with Clint as they headed toward Sharps.

They'd entered into Montana and could feel the difference almost immediately. The trees seemed to have closed in around them in spots, but the sky opened up into a deep blue expanse that made it hard to believe it was the same one hanging over the rest of the country. Normally, Clint would take a little time to enjoy a sight like that. For now, he just wanted to get where he was going and get some rest.

All too quickly, the sun dropped below the horizon and the stars flickered into the sky. The darkness dropped on them like a thick black tarp, and soon they could barely see the trail five feet in front of them.

"Where is this town?" Willow asked.

"Not much farther," Clint replied. "It's been a while, but I know we've got to be almost there."

"Do you remember the way with your eyes closed?"

He pulled back on the reins and let out a resigned breath. "No."

"Then I think we should stop until morning."

As much as he hated to admit it, she was right. Clint hadn't been able to stop thinking about the faces of those other prisoners since he'd left that camp. The longer he took to get them out of there, the longer those slavers had to inflict whatever pain they had in store.

Just then, Clint felt a hand on his shoulder.

"You're doing all you can," Willow said into his ear. "And you won't be any good to anyone if you're not rested."

Reflexively, Clint patted Willow's hand. "We'll stop, but we're heading out at first light."

"Of course."

Considering the amount of trouble they had in finding a spot to make camp, Clint had to admit that riding any further would have been plain stupid. Not only was it difficult to see the terrain, but it would have been next to impossible to spot any of the slavers' scouts if the riders were even a little skilled at doing their job.

Even after their eyes had adjusted to the dark, the shadows were damn near impenetrable. Clint was lucky to find a clear spot in the middle of a patch of bushes, which would make sneaking up on them impossible. Of course, if the scouts carried rifles, that would change things. Clint decided he would have a much easier time sleeping if he just didn't think along those lines.

They gathered up some wood, but only enough to make a fire that was barely more than a collection of sparks. The embers didn't give them much in the way of light, but it warmed their hands once the night's chill had set in.

"Looks like it's cold beans and beef jerky for supper," Clint said. "Sorry about that."

Willow smiled and bit into a piece of leathery meat. "Considering that I am eating this as a free woman, it tastes just fine."

"Really? Well, how about a nice vintage to wash it down?" Clint asked as he handed over his canteen. "I just filled this up yesterday."

She laughed and took a sip of water. After a few moments, Willow asked, "Why are you doing this?"

"We've got to eat."

"No. I mean going through all this trouble to trap those men. Did you lose somebody?"

"No, but that doesn't mean I should just sit back and let everyone else suffer. The way I see it, men like this are the worst kind of filth. I wouldn't be able to look at myself in a mirror if I just let that filth do what it pleases when I could have done something about it."

"You may get hurt. Or . . . worse."

Clint nodded slowly. "A man can die plenty of ways. I've known famous gunfighters that have fallen off their horses to break their necks or got shot in the back when hanging a picture. Neither of those were exactly what they had in mind when they thought about how they'd meet their maker. Since you can't choose how you're going to go, you might as well not be afraid of it. You'll go when it's your time. That's it."

"So you don't fear death?"

"There's no point in it."

She smiled and nodded. "You are a wise man."

"If I was a wise man, I never would have picked up so many scars along the way."

They both laughed a bit, which helped to chase away some of the shadows since the fire wasn't up to the task. After that bit of chatter, the night felt a little brighter and even the food went down a little easier.

"I think I might be able to brew a bit of coffee without building up too much more of a fire," Clint offered.

Willow shook her head and handed back his canteen. "I can hardly keep my eyes open, but thank you, Clint." She looked at him for a few more seconds as if she was committing every line of his face to memory. "Thank you for everything."

With that, she stretched out on the ground and rested her head upon her arms. Her body curled around the sputtering excuse for a campfire as if it was a comforting, roaring flame. She had a contented expression on her face as she closed her eyes and drifted off to sleep.

Clint stretched out his legs so his boots were beside the fire and his back was against a half-buried log. The canteen was cool as it sat upon his stomach and the wind brushed easily over his face. If not for the circumstances surrounding them, it would have been a genuinely peaceful night.

Willow's skin was the color of perfectly brewed tea and her eyes carried an undeniable strength. Her arms and legs were finely muscled, but her body still had plenty of soft, feminine curves. Her coal-black hair had been loosed from its braid to frame her face in a way that made Clint want to reach out and brush it back.

Instead, he pulled his hat down, crossed his arms over his chest, and tried to get some rest.

TWENTY

He crept up to Willow as she lay on the ground sleeping contentedly. It was the darkest time of the night where it was unclear whether it was still night or early morning. The sun was just below the horizon, but it still felt like it would be a long time before it showed its face.

Easing up closer, he could hear the sound of her breathing. A little bit closer, and he could feel the heat from her body and see every little squirm as she shifted every now and then to get a little more comfortable. By the time his hand was brushing along the back of her leg, he could feel his own body touching hers.

Willow's eyes came open and she twisted around. When she saw the stranger's face, her mouth opened to scream.

The man was covered in dirt and had a crooked, leering smile. His hand was strong and quick as it slapped against her mouth to keep that scream from breaking the dark silence of the night.

"Easy now, squaw," the man hissed. "No need to make any fuss."

Willow's body began to thrash against the stranger as well as the ground as she tried to get away. Her hips knocked over the little pile of ashes that were the remains of the campfire, sending a black, powdery mist into the air.

"I ain't gonna hurt ya," the stranger said as he caught one of Willow's wrists and pressed it to the ground. "That is, unless you don't stop kickin'. Just take what I got to give ya and this'll go real nice."

When Willow used her free hand to slap him, the stranger stopped for a moment and then smiled. The more she pounded against his shoulder and chest or tried to kick at him, the more interested he became in tugging at her skirts.

Willow balled up her fist and put more muscle behind her punches. One even landed on the stranger's jaw and caused him to pull in a sharp breath.

"I like a squaw with fire," he said as he delivered a savage punch to her stomach, which doubled her over and drove all the strength from her body. "Do that again, darlin'. I think I like it."

The stranger stuck out his jaw and nearly got his head knocked from his shoulders by a punch coming from the other side. The impact was enough to knock him away from Willow and send him sprawling onto his back.

"What's the matter?" Clint asked from the shadows. "I thought you said you liked that."

Flipping over so he could get on his hands and knees, the stranger searched the darkness with wild eyes. His hand darted to his boot and came back wrapped around the bone handle of a menacing blade. By this time, he'd found Clint squatting next to one of the nearby bushes.

"We been lookin' for this here squaw," the stranger hissed. "She belongs to us. This ain't your concern."

Clint merely shook his head and lifted himself into a crouch in a way that made him look like a cobra rearing up from the bushes.

"I'll kill you, mister," the stranger said with a little less venom in his tone.

"You'll try."

With that, Clint lunged forward with both arms outstretched. His left hand grabbed for the stranger's knife hand, but the other man quickly pulled it away. Clint's right hand got ahold of the stranger's jacket and closed tightly around it.

The stranger was a wiry cuss who squirmed within his jacket like a snake trying to shed a skin that was one size too big. Clint's momentum took both men to the ground, but it was the stranger who hit the hardest. Both shoulders slammed into the dirt, driving a good portion of the breath from his lungs.

As he tried to get a better grip on the stranger, Clint thought about all the others that could be making their way to the campsite at that very moment. He half-expected to feel someone knock the back of his head with a gun handle, or just put a bullet through his back and be done with it. Until any of those things happened, however, Clint could only worry about the threat right in front of him.

With a snap of his elbow, the stranger brought his arm around like a whip. His fist twisted along the way to bring the blade of his knife sailing toward Clint's throat. It cut through the air and flashed in the corner of Clint's eye, giving him less than a heartbeat to do something about it.

All Clint could do was pull back and turn away. The stranger's hand was coming too high to be blocked and too quickly to be avoided. When Clint felt the blade bite into his skin, it wasn't much of a surprise.

The stranger grinned at the sight of Clint's blood and brought his knife around to draw some more. This time, his target wasn't off his guard and his arm was stopped by a strong, solid block.

Clint glared at the stranger as he felt the warm trickle of blood running down his neck. He'd managed to get his own arm in the way of the stranger's, so now it was a race to see who could move the fastest from there.

Repositioning himself so he could get up on one knee, the stranger tightened his fist around the knife handle. Clint was still crouching, but soon felt the stranger's leg knock into the back of his knee. The blow wasn't powerful, but it did weaken his stance just enough to give the stranger an opportunity to strengthen his own.

Once he was on his feet, the stranger put some more muscle behind his arm. Every so often, he would try to twist it one way or another, but he never pulled it back. The blade was getting closer and closer to Clint's neck. It was so close now that he could already feel what it would be like to rake it in deep and really open him up.

Clint felt the pinch of the first cut, but wasn't having any trouble breathing. That told him that the cut was superficial and nothing to get too concerned about. The stranger, on the other hand, was a real concern since he was demonstrating some experience with his blade.

When Clint would shift one way, the stranger shifted another.

When Clint tried to reverse his hold and get the knife away from its owner, the stranger would twist just enough to foil the attempt.

As the struggle tipped more in the stranger's favor, the ugly smile on the stranger's face grew like an infection.

"I'll be takin' that squaw," the stranger grunted. "Whether you like it or not."

Narrowing his eyes, Clint swung at the stranger's face with his free hand. In a flicker of motion, the stranger's other hand snapped out to take hold of Clint's wrist. Clint could feel the other man's bony fingers wrapping around his wrist, and almost got free.

Almost, but not quite.

The stranger's grip cinched in with a surprising amount

of strength, preventing Clint from doing anything else with that arm.

Suddenly, Willow appeared behind the stranger with Clint's coffeepot clutched in both hands. She reared it back to swing the pot at the stranger's head, but was stopped short by a quick mule kick.

"Hold up, darlin'. Your turn's comin'."

When Clint's eyes darted to follow Willow as she dropped to the ground, he spotted another skinny figure approaching from the shadows. Although he didn't recognize the man's face, Clint could most definitely make out the pistol clutched in his fist.

The moonlight glinted off the gunman's eyes as they flicked between Clint and Willow. He looked like a hungry wolf that didn't know which bit of meat to tear off first.

TWENTY-ONE

Clint gritted his teeth as his mind raced. He'd seen the gunman creeping up to Willow, but couldn't do anything about it until he'd finished with the knife-wielding stranger. Even then, it could very well be too late.

Grinning as if he knew exactly what Clint was thinking, the stranger shifted his weight so he could get a better angle with his arm.

Clint pushed his arm forward, forcing the blade a little farther back, but the stranger only pushed back. Clint applied more muscle to shove the knife away, and it still kept coming.

Finally, Clint made a move that took the stranger completely by surprise. Without warning, he let up in his struggle and allowed the stranger's arm to push in toward his neck. Not only did it catch the stranger off his guard, but it threw him off balance since he'd been leaning with almost all his weight in that direction.

Once Clint felt the stranger falling forward, he shifted his own weight and turned to one side. The blade brushed past him again, but this time it didn't even break his skin as it passed by.

The stranger stumbled forward. By the time he realized he was falling, it was too late for him to stop himself. Clint had already twisted out of the way, gotten his hand around the other side of the stranger's arm, and guided it as he fell.

Once more, the knife sliced through the air, but it headed straight toward a tree at the edge of the campsite. The blade dug into the bark and wedged in deep until it was completely stuck. That left the stranger leaning forward and Clint standing right beside him.

Clint snapped his knee up and drove it into the stranger's gut. He then slammed his elbow down on the back of the stranger's neck with more than enough force to snap it like a twig. Even before the stranger's body could drop, Clint plucked the knife from the tree, turned at the waist, and flung it through the air.

The blade flashed with a bit of reflected moonlight as it made one complete spin before burying itself deep into the chest of the man carrying the pistol.

Gaping in stunned silence, the gunman froze in his spot. One hand was still reaching down to Willow and the other was still clutching his weapon. He reached up to feel the knife's handle protruding from his chest before dropping to his knees and crumpling onto his side.

Willow was still trying to shake off the punch she'd taken from the first stranger, and let out a little yelp when she saw the body of the second. Rather than scream, she pressed her hand to her mouth and scooted away.

Clint was crouching over the first stranger and feeling for a pulse. There was no heartbeat and he didn't even have to wonder about the second one.

"Are you all right?" he whispered.

Willow looked around and didn't calm down until she saw that Clint had been the one to ask that question. Keeping her hand over her mouth, she nodded.

"I think these are some of those scouts we've been following."

"That one was one of the men that found my village," she said through her fingers while looking down at the man with the knife in his chest.

When Clint rushed over to the second body, he saw Willow jump away reflexively. He pulled the knife from the man's chest and held it at the ready as he looked over every last inch of the bushes surrounding the camp.

"Wait here," he said. "I'm going to look for any more of them."

Willow jumped for Clint to grab him with both hands. "Please don't leave me."

"I'll be back," he said while taking her hands off him. "I just need to know if these men were acting alone or if there's more lurking about. Stay here and keep quiet. If anyone but me comes at you, use this."

Willow's hand was trembling as she took the gun that Clint handed her. Although he knew she was scared, Clint felt better with her holding the pistol rather than the stranger who'd had it before her.

"I'll let you know when I'm coming back," he said quickly. "If you don't hear my voice when you hear other footsteps headed this way, get ready to pull that trigger."

She gave him a few quick nods before watching Clint charge back into the bushes.

For a few very long minutes, Willow crouched in the darkness holding that dead man's gun.

She twitched at every sound she heard, whether it was the snap of a twig or the chirp of an insect.

Soon, her heart stopped pounding in her chest and her breaths were coming at regular intervals. By the time she heard someone rushing through the foliage toward her, she was almost back to normal.

Preparing herself for the worst, she took hold of her gun and sighted along its barrel. All she needed to do to convince herself that she could take a man's life was think back to how it had felt when that first stranger's hands had been groping her.

"It's Clint. Don't shoot."

Those words couldn't have sounded better to Willow at that moment. When she heard them, she let out the breath she'd been holding and lowered the pistol.

"There are a few more riders out there, but they're a ways off," Clint said in a rush. "We need to get out of here right now."

"What about them?" Willow asked as she glanced down at the two still forms that she'd been trying to ignore while she'd been alone with them. "Are we just going to leave them here?"

"I'm going to see to it that they're not found right away, but that's about all. We don't have time for anything else."

Willow gathered up their things and collected the horses while Clint busied himself with the cleanup.

Thankfully, the ground was fairly easy to move at that time of year. Clint managed to dig a couple trenches, roll the bodies into them, and cover them up in a short amount of time. When he climbed onto Eclipse's back, all he left behind was a pile of ash and two lumps covered in leaves.

"Come on," he said to Willow, who was still standing in her spot. "It's time to go."

He couldn't believe his eyes when he saw her turn her back to him and walk away. As much as Clint wanted to shout for her to come to him, he didn't want to bring those other scouts straight to them. Before he was forced to climb down and run after her, Clint saw Willow walk back into sight.

She wasn't alone.

"I think I'll take this one," she said while nodding toward one of the pair of horses she was leading by the reins.

Clint had seen the scouts' horses before, but had been too busy searching for more dangerous game to pay them much attention. "They'll run off or be found by the rest. We don't need to worry."

"I'm more worried about them being found," Willow said. "If they are, then the others will know something happened to those two."

"All right. Fine. Let's just get moving."

Willow hopped onto the first horse's back and wrapped the second one's reins around the saddle horn.

"The other scouts are blocking our way, so we'll need to take the long way into Sharps," Clint explained. "That means we won't be able to get there as soon as I expected."

"I'm ready, Clint," Willow said as she tucked the pistol into her belt. "Lead the way."

TWENTY-TWO

They rode all morning and through the afternoon.

Clint rarely took his spyglass from his eye as he kept watch on the scouts. A few times, Clint spotted Ka'lanu among the scouts, but wasn't about to get close enough for Willow to use her signal to call to her brother. He still wanted to believe that the Cherokee had his heart in the right place.

It was those others that Clint wasn't so sure about.

Rather than approach Sharps from the south, Clint and Willow rode to the east, overshooting the spot where they should have turned by more than five miles. By the time they'd doubled back and started riding in the proper direction, the sun was once again making its way to the western horizon.

Clint stood up in his stirrups and gazed in all directions with the spyglass. "I don't see them," he said.

"How are they supposed to know where we are?" Willow asked. "I don't even think I know anymore."

Collapsing the spyglass and putting it into his saddlebag, Clint said, "That's the point. If you're that confused, just think how those others must feel."

"Maybe they are just following us as we ride in circles. My brother would be able to keep tracking us no matter how we tried to run."

"That is if he knew exactly where to pick up the trail and if I hadn't been doing everything possible to cover it up. Besides, if your brother knows they're after you, he should be steering them in the wrong direction."

"But he isn't," Willow said quietly. "Otherwise, we would be in that town by now."

Clint looked over at her and gave her the most comforting smile he could manage. "I'd wager that if your brother knew what those other two tried to do last night, he would still be tearing them to pieces. If anything, he just found out after the fact. Maybe, he didn't know about it at all. Either way, it doesn't do us any good to speculate."

"Good, because it is making my head hurt."

"Then let's stop for the night."

"No," she snapped. "We've wasted too much time. Those wagons are still moving!"

"At their fastest, those wagons move at the same pace our horses walk. Even with the sidestepping, I'd say we're still ahead of them. Besides, we don't even know if they've decided to stop along the way."

"I guess there's nothing for us to do besides what we're already doing."

"I must be getting tired," Clint said. "Because that made perfect sense to me."

Willow smiled and climbed down from her saddle. "I'll collect the firewood so you can rest."

Clint would have objected, but she was already off and gathering before his boots hit the dirt. He dug out some supplies and tied off the horses. When Willow returned, he made another paltry excuse for a fire and handed out some more jerky.

"I'll be looking forward to getting a hot meal when we get to town," he said.

"And no coffee." Glancing at him with a shrug, she added, "No offense."

"None taken."

They ate their food and drank their water as the sun's light faded from the sky. By the time the stars were making their appearance, Clint and Willow were sitting side by side. The sound of a small creek nearby made a little trickle in the background as the air began to fill with the music of a thousand crickets.

"I wanted to thank you for what you did," Willow said.

"You took care of that a while ago."

"Not for what you did when those two men nearly . . ." She trailed off without completing the sentence. After forcing the memory to the back of her mind, she continued. "Thank you again, Clint."

"No problem. I'm sure you'd help me out if you could."

"I would. But right now, there's something else I can do." As she said that, Willow eased closer to him until she was kneeling directly in front of him. Her legs folded up underneath her body and her torso remained perfectly straight so she could look directly into Clint's eyes.

Although Clint could feel the meaning in her gaze, he kept himself from reacting to it too quickly. "I told you there's no need to thank me," he said.

"This isn't about that anymore. This is about what I want. And I think," she added while leaning forward to place her lips almost upon Clint's, "that you want it too."

Clint didn't need to say a word to answer the question in her eyes. He let his lips do his talking when he leaned forward the rest of the way so he could finish the kiss that she'd started.

Willow's mouth tasted like clean water and her lips were warm and soft. She kissed Clint gently at first, but soon let the fire that had been burning deep within her take hold and guide her hands toward Clint's body. She reached out to slide one hand along Clint's knee while the other hand drifted toward his chest.

Soon, Clint found him reaching for her as well. The moment he wrapped one arm around Willow's back, she melted into his embrace and allowed herself to be pulled in closer. Supporting her head with one hand, Clint felt her thick black hair spilling along his arm. The soft sound of her moans drifted into his ears as he nibbled a little bit on her lower lip.

"Are you certain those scouts have moved on?" she asked breathlessly.

"I haven't seen much of them all day."

"Good," she replied while slipping out of her clothes. "Because I want you all to myself for a while."

TWENTY-THREE

At that moment, Clint was able to put everything else out of his mind. He knew for a fact that the scouts had moved north quite a while ago, which was why he'd picked this spot to camp. Otherwise, he never would have allowed them to take a rest at all.

Now that they were there, together, Clint felt as if there was no other spot in the world that mattered. At least, that allowed him to relax long enough for his nerves to stop jumping under his skin.

Willow shrugged out of her blouse and let it drop to the ground. Reaching behind her head, she loosened the braids and shook out the long, flowing strands of black hair. It spilled over her shoulders and came down all the way to the upper portion of her stomach, parting just enough to reveal the firm slopes of her breasts. They were capped with small, dark nipples, which were already erect.

Hooking her thumbs into the waistband of her skirt, she pulled it down and wriggled out of it before Clint could lift a finger. She kicked it behind her so that she was now completely naked in front of him. For a moment, she looked at him with a bit of shyness on her face. That soon passed and she leaned forward to once again place her lips upon Clint's.

This time, there was more passion in their kiss. Clint felt her hands envelop his face to hold him in place as she eased her lips apart to taste him with her tongue. The moment her tongue entered his mouth, Willow began to moan softly and press herself against him with renewed urgency.

Clint couldn't get out of his clothes fast enough. He pulled open his shirt and kicked off his jeans without one bit of the grace that Willow had shown when she'd undressed. She smiled as she watched him, however, and was more than happy to tend to him once he was ready.

The cool air wrapped around them, brushing Willow's hair to one side while she climbed into Clint's lap. After settling on top of him, she wrapped her legs around his waist and lowered herself onto his rigid penis. Her arms were wrapped around his neck and she closed her eyes while slowly taking him inside her.

Clint was sitting with his legs outstretched. He cupped her firm little backside in both hands to guide her until he was buried deep inside her moist embrace. Sliding one arm along her back, Clint used his other hand to lift her until she began rocking back and forth on top of him.

His cock slid in and out of her in a slow rhythm. Willow leaned forward, pressing her pert breasts against Clint's chest. Her hair draped over his shoulders to tickle his back. Soon, she started to grind her hips in a slow circle, adding another layer of sensation to their lovemaking. When she'd found a good spot, she kept herself there and began pumping her hips a little faster.

Clint leaned back slowly, allowing her to shift to the new position. She took to it naturally and was soon arching her back on top of him. He watched as she placed both hands flat upon his chest and kept riding him. Her hair swirled slowly with the breeze and her breasts wiggled ever so slightly when their bodies collided.

Taking hold of her hips in both hands, Clint kept her still while he began thrusting up into her. Willow was reluctant to stop moving at first, but soon broke into a wide smile as she felt his hard cock thrusting into her again and again.

It wasn't long before Willow leaned back even farther. She reached back with both hands to brace herself against Clint's legs. The slope of her body was a smooth, curving arc. Clint was given a perfect view along that arc, which led right up to the pert breasts and fully erect nipples.

Her body writhed back and forth in time to his thrusts. Soon, her breaths quickened and the muscles in her stomach began to tense with anticipation. Clint reached out to slide his hand along the front of her body until his thumb was gently massaging her clitoris. From there, it only took a few more thrusts before Willow was in the grip of a powerful climax.

She brought her hand to her mouth and bit down on her finger to keep from crying out. When Clint sat up again, she wrapped her arms around him and put her mouth to his ear. That way, when she let out her quiet, satisfied moan, it sent a shiver along his spine.

Clint lifted her up and set her on her back so he could position himself between her legs. His cock slid into her once more and he glided in and out of her in smooth strokes. It wasn't long before he felt his own orgasm approaching and he kept pumping until he exploded inside her.

Willow let out another groan and was barely able to keep it from echoing into the sky over their heads. She took hold of his hips, preventing him from leaving her.

For a moment, Clint stayed put just to see what she had in mind. Then, when he felt her tightening around him, her plan became perfectly obvious.

The muscles between her legs flexed in a quick rhythm

that echoed the previous rhythm of their bodies. Soon, she'd coaxed him back to a full erection and was grinding her hips against him in a series of quick circles. Willow watched Clint's face the entire time, grinning when she saw his eyes roll back as a new wave of pleasure swept through him.

Before he knew what was happening, Clint was thrusting into her again. He was acting on pure instinct, allowing the animal in him to take control and enjoy the carnal pleasures that Willow was offering. When his next climax came, Willow followed right along with him.

Together, they grabbed hold of one another and wrapped themselves into a tangle of arms and legs. Clint's hips thrust with more and more power, spurred on by Willow's insistent whispers into his ear.

"Harder," she pleaded. "Don't stop. Don't stop."

Clint had no intention of stopping.

By the time they'd both been pushed beyond the point of no return, they practically collapsed.

Clint fell asleep gazing up at the stars with Willow curled up beside him.

TWENTY-FOUR

They awoke at dawn, bright-eyed and raring to go. They ate a quick breakfast and were on their way to Sharps as if they'd been shot out of a cannon. Previously, Clint had figured on getting into town by early evening. They were riding through the center of it by late afternoon.

"I didn't see the wagons," Willow said.

"I wouldn't expect to see them yet. If your brother does his part, he should be on his way to give his report right now or real soon."

"I haven't seen him either."

Clint nodded, trying to make it seem as if things were all going according to plan. "Keep your eyes open. If we don't catch sight of him soon, we'll catch up to him later. For right now, let's get settled and take it from there. First of all, we need some supplies."

Looking around at the crooked streets and run-down structures that seemed to be one stiff breeze from falling over, Willow scowled and said, "I don't like the looks of this place. Some of these men remind me of the ones we're hiding from."

"Keep your head down and try not to look at any of them directly. At least, until we get somewhere we can put up our horses."

"How much farther is that?"

"About ten paces."

They were riding around a corner, which led them straight to a small barn situated more or less by itself. The town was more of a collection of stray buildings that all seemed to have been pieced together by the same inept carpenter. The door to the barn came open noisily and the two rode inside.

"Stay here," Clint said. "I'll be right back."

Willow nodded and began taking the saddles off all three horses.

By the time Clint walked out of the barn, he'd already attracted the attention he'd been hoping for. At first, however, he wasn't certain he would survive the encounter.

"You'd better not have taken anything from my barn, mister, or you won't live to regret it."

The threat came from a slender woman with long brown hair. She was dressed in a light purple dress and holding a shotgun as if she had every intention of using it. The stern expression on her face left nothing to the imagination in that regard.

Once she got a look at who was walking toward her with hands held high, the stern expression on her face turned into a smile.

"Clint? Is that you?"

"It sure is. How you doing, Abby?"

Although she seemed to have forgotten about the shotgun she held, Abby had yet to lower it. She rushed forward and almost drove the shotgun's barrel into Clint's gut before he was able to swipe it away.

"Sorry about that," she said as she lowered the shotgun.

"I've grown to be a little more cautious since the last time we met."

"If you call that cautious, I'd hate to see your version of suspicious."

She showed him a wry grin and replied, "You may have raised hell the last time you were here, but there's plenty more wicked souls out there to come in after you left." After letting him wait for a moment, Abby added, "Things have been a lot better since you drove out those claim jumpers, but we still get our share of trouble."

"Well, it looks like you can handle your share. How's the store coming along?"

"Still where it was the last time you were here." Reaching out with one hand, she slid her palm along Clint's chest. "I see everything else with you is still in its proper place."

"You've gotten a little bolder since the last time."

"After those nights we had, there isn't much for either of us to be shy about."

They let their eyes linger on each other for a few moments before pulling themselves away.

"So what brings you back to Sharps?" Abby asked. "Looks like you're not alone."

"I'm not. And I'm expecting some others to be stopping by. Actually, they may have already passed through."

Abby was leaning forward to get a look into the barn. Once she saw Willow, she glanced back toward Clint. "Still have a taste for the dark-haired ones, I see?"

Clint grinned, but bit his tongue.

"Don't fret it," Abby said with a wink. "A little competition never hurt anyone. Bring her along. I can get you something to eat and you can tell me about these friends of yours."

"Thanks, Abby. You're sure it's no trouble?"

"None at all. Any friend of yours is a friend of mine."

TWENTY-FIVE

"Abby, this is Willow," Clint said.

Abby extended her hand and gave Willow a friendly smile. "That's a pretty name."

Willow nodded and sat down on one of the two benches next to the long table that took up a good portion of Abby's dining room. The house was one of the sturdier structures in town, but that wasn't saying a whole lot considering the rest of Sharps. The place was clean and comfortable, however, which was a whole lot better than sitting on the ground.

"I met Abby a while ago when I settled a matter here," Clint explained.

"Filled the streets with gunfire," Abby said. "At least, that's the way folks have been telling it ever since. As usual, the truth is somewhere in the middle." While pouring water for herself and her guests, she asked, "So how many others are you expecting?"

"Two or three," Clint replied. "Maybe a few more."

"Don't you know for certain?"

"Not exactly. We're part of a caravan and scouting ahead to make sure the trail is clear. There's plenty of scouts in the whole group, but I don't know exactly how many found their way here."

"Considering all the new girls that have been working along Solomon Street, I wouldn't be surprised if they all found their way there."

When she got only half a chuckle from Clint in response to her joke, Abby sat down and studied the other two carefully. "Is there something you're not telling me? The two of you look pretty grim."

"There's been some trouble along the way," Clint said.

Abby nodded. "You seem to attract that sort of thing, Clint."

"Hopefully, it's nothing that will have followed us here, but there's no way to be sure. I really just need to have a word with the others to see how things are looking."

"Well, there have been a few strangers coming through lately," Abby announced. "There's usually someone coming along. After all, I wasn't lying about the girls on Solomon Street. But the ones I'm thinking of stick out from the rest."

"Why's that?"

"Because they caught the eye of some of our local peacekeepers." Shaking her head, Abby let out a weary sigh. "I'm using those words loosely since this town's peacekeepers aren't much more than shifty landowners with guns."

"When are you folks going to get some law in this town?"

"As soon as someone steps up for the task, Clint. Ever since the last time you blew through here, there hasn't been any trouble that we couldn't handle. Some men around here just get a little overly anxious when they see a couple Indians ride down the street. No offense, Willow."

Willow brushed off the apology as if she hadn't even

heard what brought it on. "What two are you talking about?"

"They arrived yesterday. Both of them were Indians. One was a rough-looking sort with scars on his neck. Big fellow. The other was pretty big as well, but with longer hair and things in it. You know, braided in there."

"What kind of things?"

Abby shrugged and replied, "Beads, I guess. Maybe some gold."

Clint nodded. "That sounds like the men we're looking for. Any idea where they are?"

"Try Solomon Street. That's where the only two hotels in town are and I know for a fact none of the folks around here would rent a room to them." Abby winced and looked again at Willow. "You're welcome here, you understand."

Willow nodded. The smile on her face couldn't have possibly been wiped away by just those stray words. "I understand."

"I could take you down there and ask around about your friends," Abby offered.

"No need for any of that," Clint said. "If you could just point me in the right direction, that would be fine."

"Looking to surprise these fellas?"

"Something like that."

Abby nodded and motioned for him to follow her. The two of them stepped to a window, where Abby leaned in close to the glass and dropped her voice to a whisper. "You know you can trust me, Clint."

"I know."

"Then why does it seem like there's something going on that you're not sharing with me?"

"Because there are some dangerous men involved," Clint replied. "I'd rather not get you too deeply involved if I can help it."

"Are these really friends you're after?"

"That remains to be seen." Clint shifted so his back was

to Willow and Abby was all he could see. Her eyes fixed upon him and her full lips were even softer than he remembered. "If everything goes smoothly, we should be in and out of here in no time at all. If things don't go smoothly, it could get rough. Maybe even rougher than I want to think about."

It took a moment, but Abby was able to read between the lines. It seemed that Clint trusted Willow well enough, but he wasn't certain if she could handle the bumps that might be ahead of them on this road. Having seen how rough things could get where Clint was concerned, Abby didn't mind taking his word for it and keeping at arm's length. At least for now.

"All right then," Abby said in a voice that was only slightly louder than the whispers they'd been using previously. "The place you're after is called Line's Emporium."

"That's on Solomon Street?"

Abby nodded. "It wasn't here the last time you were in town, but it's awfully popular. I know at least one of those others you're with headed there. The rest shouldn't be far away."

Willow stood up. "We should go now then."

"I agree," Clint said.

"Can you tell me where you folks are headed?" Abby asked. "Just in case I don't get a chance to say good-bye?"

"The wagons are headed into Oregon," Clint said. He hated to lie to Abby, but the less she knew about the truth, the less reason there would be for any of those slavers to come after her on the off chance they looked in her direction.

Judging by the look in Abby's eyes, she didn't believe him anyway.

TWENTY-SIX

It was a good thing that Abby gave him more precise directions to Line's Emporium. Clint might have overlooked the place since the only letters that were still visible on the chipped, weatherbeaten sign out front labeled the place as LI S E P R UM.

Missing letters notwithstanding, the sign was lit up by torches on either side of it as if it marked the entrance into the Promised Land. Small windows opened along the sides of the thick building, displaying women in various states of undress like pies cooling on a sill.

Willow turned away from the women leaning out of the windows, some of whom were propositioning her as well as Clint. "So this place wasn't here the last time you were in town?" she asked.

"Nope," Clint replied while tipping his hat to a chunky redhead with a plunging neckline. "I certainly would have remembered all of this."

"My brother would never be in such a place. We should look somewhere else."

Rather than try to educate her on the weaknesses of every man, Clint let Willow think her brother was above all that. He patted her on the shoulder and steered her toward the bustling saloon. "I know, but maybe the other ones are here and your brother is just keeping an eye on them."

Willow shook her head at the sarcasm in Clint's voice, but let it pass.

Inside, Line's Emporium was an even bigger mess than it was on the outside. There weren't two tables that looked alike, mainly because most of them were actually overturned barrels or crates stacked on top of each other.

Stools of all shapes and sizes littered the floor and the bar was actually a collection of planks laid over a set of rails, covered with a bunch of old sheets. When he got a look at it, Clint had to shake his head.

"I thought the Holdout was a sorry excuse for a watering hole," he groaned. "This place makes it not seem so bad."

"It looks bad to me," Willow groaned. Suddenly, her face brightened up with a beaming smile. "I see him!"

Clint's hand snapped out to push down the finger Willow was about to point. "Tell me where he is and keep walking. We're already attracting too much attention."

"Over there in the corner. See him?"

Clint saw him all right. The Cherokee was leaning his elbows against a table in the back of the place, talking to a blond girl in her late teens who was too well dressed to be a waitress. Since there was no stage in the place, Clint had one more guess as to what Ka'lanu's companion did for a living. Since he couldn't blame the man for choosing the pretty blonde, Clint kept his opinions to himself and let Willow form her own.

Clint did his best to let out a short, crisp whistle that sounded similar to the one made by Willow's signal. It was barely enough to make it through the noise in the saloon, and it was close enough to the original to catch Ka'lanu's attention. The Cherokee's head perked up and he immediately started looking around.

The moment her brother was looking at her, Willow gave him a wave.

"All right," Clint said. "He sees you. Now come along with me and keep your head down."

Willow did just that and made her way to a table, which appeared to be an old serving tray nailed to the top of a post. Ka'lanu stepped up beside her in a matter of minutes. He announced his presence to his sister by giving her hand a warm squeeze.

"It's good to see you," Ka'lanu said. "I wasn't sure if you were still alive." Looking at Clint, he asked, "Was there any trouble getting here?"

"Judging by the first part of your statement, I'd guess you know damn well there was trouble."

Ka'lanu nodded solemnly. "A few of the men took off on their own. They said they'd picked up another trail and left before I could stop them. I tried to follow, but . . ."

"You did the right thing in letting them go," Clint said.

But Ka'lanu didn't seem to hear him. "Did they hurt you?" he asked Willow. "Did they try to—"

"You did the right thing," Clint interrupted. "Your sister's fine. What you need to worry about is helping us save the rest of those prisoners."

For a moment, Ka'lanu looked angered by the interruption. Then he nodded and said, "You are right. Tell me of your plan."

"First I need to know about the other scouts. How many are left?"

"There were five of us who rode out to check this trail. Now, there are three."

"Can you trust any of those other two?" Clint asked.

After a moment of consideration, Ka'lanu shrugged. "Maybe one. Definitely not the other."

"Is there any way for you to be certain? We don't have

any slack where that's concerned and we sure don't have enough time to work through every doubt you may have."

"It depends on what you need," Ka'lanu replied. "One of the others would be trustworthy if I told him we were working to replace the big belly. Other than that, I'm not so sure."

"Fair enough." Clint looked around to see if any of the nearby drinkers or working girls were staring a bit too hard in their direction. As far as he could tell, everyone was too wrapped up in their own affairs to notice much else. "Where are the other scouts now?"

"They are with the women they paid for," the Cherokee replied. "I don't know how much longer it will be before they return. You'd better tell me what you need me to do quickly."

"Not here," Clint said. "Will staying through the night be a problem?"

Ka'lanu shook his head. "We weren't going to ride out until sunrise."

"Good. Then meet us a few hours from now at a barn a few streets over. We should have enough privacy to go over everything there. Come alone and make sure you're not followed."

Ka'lanu nodded and stood up. He reached out to rub his sister's chin and show her a warm smile. After that, he turned his back to her and quickly headed to the opposite end of the saloon. By the time he looked over his shoulder again, Clint and Willow were gone.

TWENTY-SEVEN

Clint made the rounds and quickly discovered that Abby had been right about Sharps. There was still no law and the locals were ready and willing to take care of themselves. What she didn't know was how badly the town needed some official peacekeepers. Since he lived and died by being able to read people with sometimes no more than a glance, he could feel the heat in the air that had nothing to do with the time of year.

Men walked the streets not only wearing guns, but itching to use them. Their eyes darted toward any sound at all and their hands twitched toward the holsters at their sides or the shotguns held under their arms. The ones that didn't fall into that category were too drunk to realize how close they were to being shot just for belching too loud.

Clint patrolled the streets looking for one of the other scouts. Although he hadn't seen the others except through his spyglass from almost a mile away, Clint knew he would recognize them the moment they crossed his path. There was something in those slavers' eyes that set them apart from the trigger-happy vigilantes that had taken over that town. It was a genuine dangerousness that came from taking lives instead of just bragging about it.

While Clint circled the barn and walked the nearby streets, he couldn't find a trace of any slavers lurking about or watching the spot for the meeting. Clint wanted to believe that things were set to go smoothly and perfectly, but he knew better than to expect so much.

Things rarely went smoothly and they never went perfectly.

Most of the time, the best that anyone could hope for in situations like this was to come out of it alive. The safest route for Clint to take was to call in the law and let them try their luck in taking down the slavers. But Clint knew well enough that if even a few of the prisoners made it out of that in one piece, they would be very lucky.

He stood outside for another few minutes, leaning against the side of a shack that could barely support his weight. It sounded as if some people were inside, but they were arguing about something or other and didn't notice Clint standing next to the window.

Clint pulled in some air and looked up at the stars. If he didn't concern himself with everything else that was happening, it was actually a fine evening. There was a gentle breeze that cooled him as it brushed against his face. The smell of cooking fires drifted into his nose, and the piano player in some saloon was loud enough for Clint to make out the song.

It was the calm before the storm.

Clint had been through more than enough storms to recognize the quiet time for what it was. He'd also been through enough of them to know he needed to savor them while he could. No matter what anyone said about him, Clint knew better than to think he was immortal.

One of these times, he wouldn't make it through the storm. Some young gun might get a lucky shot or Clint might just run into someone far better than him.

There was always someone better out there. Clint knew that because he'd seen the look of surprise on the faces of too many men who hadn't come to grips with that fact themselves. He'd been the better man to knock plenty of cocky shooters off their perches.

Someday . . .

"Mind if I join you?"

Clint had heard the light footsteps approaching him, and had recognized them well enough that he didn't even need to look to know who was coming. Now that she was standing beside him, Clint could smell the fresh scent of her long hair.

"Sure, Willow," Clint replied. "Although we might just knock this shack over."

"Then I'll stand," she said with a grin. "Have you seen any of those other men?"

"No."

"What about my brother?"

"He's not supposed to be here for a little while yet, and he might be a little late since he's got to worry about making sure he's really alone."

Slowly, Willow stepped in front of Clint and slipped her arms around him. She squeezed him tight and then placed her lips against his so she could kiss him deeply. The moment he kissed her back, Clint felt her lips part and her tongue slip out to taste him.

The kiss was over as suddenly as it began. Willow stepped back and smiled at him.

"What was that for?" Clint asked.

"Just in case I don't get a chance like this one for a while."

"I know just what you mean." With that, Clint took her in his arms and kissed her again.

TWENTY-EIGHT

At first glance, the barn looked empty.

It had two rows of three stalls in the back with half a loft above. The rest of the space was open and cluttered with stacks of hay, bags of feed, and supplies of all kinds propped up against the wall. When the wind blew, it rattled the barn and filled the air with the creaks of old wood. Cobwebs hung from every corner like thick, unmoving smoke.

Ka'lanu walked in and stopped. He looked around to take in all these sights as his eyes adjusted to the gloom. When he didn't see anything else, his hand drifted to the gun at his side. "Is anybody here?"

A light grew in one corner until it was just enough to illuminate Clint's face. He stood leaning against one of the stalls. One hand was on the lantern's knob and the other was scratching Eclipse's ear.

"Right here, Ka'lanu," Clint replied. "Come in and shut the door behind you."

The Cherokee hurried inside and eased the barn door shut.

"Did anyone try to follow you?" Clint asked.

"They tried, but I kept them from coming here. I had to knock one of them out and drag him somewhere else."

"Like where?"

"Behind the saloon where we met before," Ka'lanu replied. "He won't be surprised to wake up with a headache there."

"Good thinking. What about the other scout that's in town?"

"He may help us. We might not want to tell him everything, but he will have no problem going against the big belly. He even brought up something like that himself."

Clint nodded. "So I guess he's on his way here?"

"Yes, but he won't be here for a little while. That gives us time to talk."

"Sure does."

"Where is my sister?"

Before Clint could say anything, Willow went against the plan by showing herself before being signaled that it was safe. She was plainly happy to see her brother, but winced the moment she caught sight of Clint's stern glare.

"I'm here," she said since it was too late to go back into hiding at the back of the stall next to Eclipse's.

Ka'lanu let out a breath and lowered his guard a bit. "Whatever we do, I want my sister to be safe."

"I agree," Clint said. "She's not to have any part in what's to come. I won't put her in sight of those wagons since she fought so hard to get away from them."

"Good. Now what do you want from me?"

Clint stepped forward and cleared away some of the loose hay that had fallen onto the floor. Using a stick, he scratched out a map similar to the one he'd shown to Mason. From there, he went through the bare bones of his plan while the Cherokee listened intently.

Ka'lanu didn't say a word while Clint talked. Instead, he soaked up everything Clint had to say while only nodding occasionally to show that he was following along.

As he went through the plan, Clint watched Ka'lanu's face to see if he could get a read on the man. But the Cherokee remained perfectly neutral. His face might have looked angry or focused depending on what Clint was expecting. His eyes were equally fixed, which made them hard to read.

Ka'lanu was thinking something, but Clint could only guess as to what it was.

After he'd gone through the overall plan, Clint waited for a moment before asking, "What do you think?"

"I can get the wagons to go through that canyon, but the scouts will be sent up to clear the tops of those rocks. If I tried to stop that, the big belly would know something was wrong."

"Don't worry about them." Clint said. "But if there's any scouts who you want to stay healthy, you might want to keep them from going up there."

Ka'lanu nodded. "There is only one."

"What I need from you is to see about getting the wagons holding those prisoners separated from the rest of the caravan. At the very least, try to get them at one end with some space between them and the rest of the group."

The Cherokee furrowed his brow and let out a slow, measured breath. "That will be hard to do."

"But is there a way for you to do it?"

After a few moments of quiet consideration, Ka'lanu nodded. "I can think of a way."

"If you're worried about anyone getting suspicious, whatever story you choose won't have to hold up long. Even if you just pull those wagons back before they get to this spot," Clint said while tapping the map scratched into the dirty floor, "that should be enough. Before anyone will get a chance to question you too much, they'll have plenty more to keep them busy."

"The big belly will not be frightened. He will send many men with guns to keep those captives from being set free."

"That's why it's so important for you to separate them from the rest."

"You will be in danger as well. More danger than you may think," Ka'lanu explained. "The big belly will send every man he has to kill you. If he succeeds, all of this will be for nothing and those women and children will be killed or sold just like before."

"They'll be killed or sold off anyway," Clint said. "They've got enough weapons to hold back an army. At least this will be something they won't be expecting."

Suddenly, Clint felt a chill run down his spine. He didn't know if he got that feeling before or after he heard the scraping of boots over his head, but he didn't waste any time trying to figure it out. Instead, he snapped his eyes toward the rickety loft and picked out the figure crouching in the shadows above the stalls.

TWENTY-NINE

"Who's there?" Clint shouted.

The figure was so small and narrow that it almost disappeared when it hunkered down a bit more and backed off.

Lowering his hand to the modified Colt at his side, Clint fixed his eyes upon the figure overhead. "I see you up there, so you might as well come down."

There were a few more scrapes and then silence.

Willow backed against the back of her stall and nervously glanced upward. "Clint, I—"

She was silenced by a quick wave from both Clint and Ka'lanu.

For a moment, the only thing that could be heard was the rustle of the wind against loose sections of the roof. Then, like a metallic snake poking its head out of its hole, a pistol barrel slipped between two boards of the loft's floor.

The moment Clint saw that gun barrel, he drew his Colt and sent a shot into the loft. He could hear a few quick steps heading toward the back of the barn, so he sent another pair of rounds aimed at the very back of the loft.

After a few more loud scrapes, the man in the loft tripped over his own feet and landed with a thump, which sent a shower of dust into the barn. Clint didn't need to ask the intruder to come down, since the boards beneath the man's feet cracked and gave way, dropping the man to the straw-covered floor.

Willow was pressed up so tightly against the back of the stall that she'd almost pushed herself through the wall.

Clint had his modified Colt aimed at the skinny man, completely ignoring the pistol that the man still held.

Ka'lanu had his gun drawn as well, but lowered it when he got a look at who'd dropped in on them. "Avery?"

"It's me," the skinny man said. "Think you can tell your friend there to lower his gun?"

Clint shook his head. "Not until I find out who the hell you are and what the hell you're doing here."

"His name is Avery," Ka'lanu said. "And he is the other scout I was telling you about."

Clint's gun arm didn't budge. "Is he the one you could trust or the one you couldn't?"

"I can trust him well enough."

Although Avery seemed to be pleased to hear that, Clint caught the trace of hesitation running underneath the Cherokee's voice.

Avery got up, stuck his gun under his belt, and dusted himself off. The scout was practically all skin and bones. He wore thick cotton pants and a shirt that wrapped around him like a sack. The hair poking out from beneath his hat seemed as if it had been picked up from the barn's floor rather than sprouting from his head.

It was hard to take Avery's smile at face value, but that might have been due to the rows of crooked, filthy teeth that he displayed. "Sorry about the entrance, but the red man here said you wanted to meet up."

"What about the gun?" Clint asked. "Did he tell you to point that at me by way of an introduction?"

"Not as such." Avery shifted on his feet and bit on his lower lip. Finally, he shrugged. "I got no excuse for that. We all get a bit overcautious doing the job we do."

"Yeah," Clint said. "I know all about the job you do."

"You ain't the law, are ya?"

"No."

"Well, then," Avery said with another filthy smile. "I suppose there ain't no reason we can't be friends. Let's start off on the right foot." He stuck his hand out to Clint. "Pleased to meet ya."

Although Clint didn't shake Avery's hand, he did ease the Colt back into its holster. "Likewise."

"Why were you spying on us?" Ka'lanu asked without even trying to hide the anger in his voice. "I told you to come here after—"

"Yeah," Avery interrupted. "But you didn't say a damn thing about trying to attack our own men. I got my grievances against Umberto, but I ain't about to kill everyone working for him. They're our friends."

"Your friends," Ka'lanu said evenly.

Clint stepped between the men before things could get any worse. "Nobody's talking about killing everyone in those wagons."

When Avery shifted his eyes to Clint, he dropped the unconvincing smile. "Then what were you two whispering about, huh? Scratching in the dirt and plotting like a couple of goddamn assassins."

"All we were talking about was separating the prisoners from the rest of the group."

"So's you could kill one bunch and not the other!"

"No," Clint said sternly. "Things won't come to that unless those slavers make it happen. And no matter who they are or how much they've paid you, they are indeed slavers." As he said that, he studied Avery's eyes.

When he'd talked to Ka'lanu about the prisoners, Clint could tell that the Cherokee truly didn't know he was a party to shipping prisoners into slavery. When he broached the same subject to Avery, Clint didn't even see a hint of surprise on the scout's dirty face.

"All I do is scout for the easiest way for all them wagons to get where they're going," Avery said. "It ain't my place to know what's in them wagons."

Willow stood up and started walking forward. Her eyes were fixed upon Avery.

"Stay out of this," Clint said. "What are you doing?"

Raising her arm, she pointed at Avery. "He's one of them."

"I know he is. We're trying to—"

"No!" Willow shouted. "He's one of the men that tried to hurt me when I was locked up in that wagon."

Ka'lanu's eyes narrowed and his entire face darkened with rage. "What did you do to her?" he asked the other scout.

Avery patted the air and backed up, struggling to come up with something to say.

As much as Clint had wanted to keep things quiet and civil, it seemed that it was too late for any of that now.

THIRTY

Before Avery could think of a way to pacify the Cherokee, Ka'lanu swung his fist. Avery ducked under the punch and staggered to one side. It was all he could do to keep his footing while trying to steer clear of both Clint and Ka'lanu.

"I didn't lay a damn finger on her," Avery insisted.

"That night before we rode out the last time," Ka'lanu snarled. "You told me you laid with a woman in camp. You said she was one of the ones that we picked up along the way."

"Yeah . . . maybe . . . well, that wasn't her!"

"Help us and make up for what you've done," Clint said quickly. It sounded weak even to him, but it was the only thing he could think of to say that wouldn't add more fuel to the fire.

"I didn't do anything!" Avery squealed in a high-pitched whine.

"Did you touch any of those prisoners?" Ka'lanu asked.

Avery stopped talking, but kept backing away. His steps

were taking him closer and closer to the front of the barn. "I don't know. Maybe once or twice, but I wasn't the only one."

"You son of a bitch," Ka'lanu growled as he ran toward Avery like a charging buffalo.

Clint forgot about everything else at that moment. The only thing on his mind was keeping Ka'lanu from getting himself hurt and making sure that Willow wasn't caught in the middle of whatever happened.

So far, neither of the men had their guns drawn. Ka'lanu was trying to get his bare hands around Avery's neck and Avery was doing his damnedest to keep that from happening. Ka'lanu was fast for a man of his size and Avery was barely able to duck under the Cherokee's arms and scuttle away.

"I've ridden with you since you came to work for Umberto," Avery said. "And you're gonna take that asshole's word over mine?"

But Ka'lanu was beyond words. His eyes had all but glazed over, and only became more focused when his arms closed around empty air. After bouncing off the wall of the barn, he wheeled around to set his eyes once again on his target.

Clint rushed up behind the Cherokee and took hold of him by both arms. "We can still use him to help us," he said quickly. "He can tell us more that will help us take these slavers down! We just need him alive if he's going to—"

Ka'lanu shook Clint off like an old coat. He didn't even need to break stride before he was once again closing in on his prey.

Avery had already bounced off one wall and was stumbling into another. His feet scrambled against the straw-covered floor and when he started to slip, he dropped like a stone rather than fight for his balance. That move caught Ka'lanu by surprise and the Cherokee's hands smashed into the wall over Avery's head.

Sinking a bit farther down, Avery pulled his knee up to his chest and lashed out with his leg. The heel of his boot pounded against Ka'lanu's knee, staggering him back a few steps.

If Ka'lanu felt any pain, he didn't show it. Instead, he gritted his teeth and forced himself to move on. The moment he put some weight down on the leg that Avery had kicked, he let out a groan and nearly fell over.

Avery smelled the Cherokee's weakness like a scavenger that had caught the scent of rotting meat. As he stood up by sliding his back against the wall, he grabbed for the gun that had been tucked under his belt.

Before Avery could complete his draw, he was forced to dive to one side as Clint came flying at him.

Clint hadn't been more than a few feet away when he'd leapt at Avery. His intention was to get to the skinny little bastard before he could make things worse and draw his gun. What he'd wound up doing was forcing Avery closer to the barn's front door and almost getting a mouthful of wall for his trouble.

Before Avery could get any time to gloat, he caught sight of more movement out of the corner of his eye. This time, he wasn't quick enough to dodge the incoming fist that was headed straight toward him.

Ka'lanu's knuckles cracked against Avery's face, sending a spray of blood as well as a few teeth into the air. Another fist followed soon after. This one caught Avery in the chest so hard that he couldn't draw in his next breath.

"We need him alive," Clint said as if he could read the bloody thoughts going through Ka'lanu's head.

The Cherokee didn't take his eyes off the other scout. As he stepped forward, he loomed over Avery while holding out one hand palm-up. "Give me your gun."

Avery was on his ass once again, propped against the wall with both hands flat against the floor. Without a moment's hesitation, he braced himself and kicked Ka'lanu's knee with both feet. When he heard the snap of separating bone, he smiled good and wide.

Clint had Avery in his sight. He drew his Colt the moment he saw the scout reach for his. Unfortunately, Ka'lanu could no longer stand on both legs and when his dislocated knee gave out, he fell directly between Clint and Avery.

"You want my gun, red man?" Avery hissed. "Here it is." With that, Avery drew his pistol and fired two shots directly into Ka'lanu's chest.

The Cherokee let out a gasping breath, but kept his eyes fixed upon Avery.

Avery watched Ka'lanu fall flat and glared into his eyes. "God damn red m . . . red ma . . ." When he was unable to finish his sentence, he seemed confused. That's when he looked down to see Ka'lanu's arm extended and his hand wrapped around the handle of a knife. The knife's blade was wedged right up under Avery's sternum.

Once Ka'lanu saw the life flicker out of Avery's eyes, he allowed himself to fall the rest of the way to land on the floor in front of him.

THIRTY-ONE

"No!" Willow shouted as she ran past Clint and dropped to her brother's side.

Clint was still standing there with his gun in hand, looking at the two dead men as if there was anything left for him to do. It had all happened so fast that Clint felt more like he'd watched it from a mile away instead of being in the thick of it.

Willow had her ear close to Ka'lanu's mouth, but whatever the Cherokee whispered was only loud enough for her to hear. Tears were streaming down her cheeks, but she made no other sound as she reached forward to close his eyes.

Clint walked over to her, still shaking his head in disbelief. "I'm so sorry. I just . . . don't know what else to say."

She stood up and walked back toward the stalls. Although it wasn't the first time he'd heard gunfire, Eclipse was still shifting restlessly and stomping at the floor.

Willow shook her head. In a way, she seemed to be doing so at Clint, but she also seemed to be shaking herself out of a trance. "It's not your fault. It's his. That filthy animal killed my brother."

"We should find Abby. She'll know how to handle whoever comes to check on those shots."

But Willow kept shaking her head.

"Come on now," Clint insisted. "We'll see that your brother is given a proper burial, but we need to make sure that we don't get on the wrong side of these local peacemakers. They strike me as the sort who shoot first and ask questions later."

"We're still going after those wagons."

"What did you say?"

Turning to look at Clint directly, Willow said, "We still need to go after those wagons, Clint."

"We can think about that later. First we need to—"

"My brother died trying to help put those horrible men in their proper place and I won't give up now. Not after the price he paid."

Clint took hold of Willow by the shoulders and looked her straight in the eye. Although she'd been facing him before, it took a moment before she truly seemed to see him there. "Listen to me," Clint said in an even tone. "I need to get in contact with Mason and come up with another plan. Your brother played a pivotal part in this and . . . well, he can't help us anymore."

Willow was so quiet for the next few moments that Clint didn't know what to expect. Her face was blank and the only movement she made was the occasional blink of her eyes. Finally, she pulled in a breath and nodded solemnly.

"You're right," she said.

"We'll think of something," Clint told her. "Right now, we need to deal with what's on our plate."

She shook her head. "No. We don't have time to come up with anything new. There's got to be a way to make this plan work."

"It's too late for that. We needed one of the scouts to direct the wagons in this direction and there aren't any scouts left. At least none that I know of, and even if there is one left somewhere, we can't bank on him steering the wagons where we need them to go."

"I'll do it."

Willow's voice was so weak that Clint didn't even hear it.

"I need to get a message to Mason," he thought out loud. "After everything that's happened we might as well just ride out to find him."

"I said I can do it," Willow repeated with renewed strength.

"Do what?"

Her eyes were growing wide and her words began to spill out of her. "We can find that other scout and let him capture me. He'll ask what happened here and I can tell him just enough to make him think the wagons should come this way."

"What could you tell them to make them do such a thing?"

"Well, I could tell them that there's a trap set and the only way around it is through that canyon."

Clint was shaking his head even before she finished talking. "They won't believe a word you tell them. More than likely, they won't even listen to anything you have to say."

"I can make them believe I know something."

"And the only way they'll think you're telling the truth is if they force it out of you. Trust me, Willow, you don't want men like this forcing anything out of you. They might not even stop once you tell them something they do believe."

That only caused her to set her jaw firmly and stand up straighter. "My brother died to put a stop to these men. I can endure some hardship if it means getting that done. Besides, they have already done enough to me. A little more won't make a difference."

"I'm not going to let you do this," Clint said as he led

her away from the bodies. "You could be tortured or killed. And after all that, you still might not get them to do one damn thing differently. Would your brother really want you to go through all that without even knowing you could make a difference?"

"Can you tell me for certain that they would have believed him?" she asked. "Can you guarantee that they would have taken my brother's route instead of what any of the other scouts suggested?"

As much as he wanted to lie to her, Clint knew it wouldn't hold up under the intensity of Willow's stare. Judging by the way she looked at him, she already knew the answer to her own question.

"Tell me this," Clint offered. "Would your brother agree to this after he risked so much to set you free?"

She hesitated for a moment and started to nod. "Maybe you're right."

"Let's just get out of here and think things through."

"I'll get the horses," Willow said with resignation. "You make sure nobody else is coming."

Clint turned toward the bodies lying at the front of the barn. He heard some light footsteps behind him and then felt his head snapping forward. Intense pain flashed for a moment, followed by a wave of numbing blackness.

He vaguely remembered drawing his pistol, but even that felt more like a dream. . . .

THIRTY-TWO

". . . and you know the rest," Clint said.

Abby nodded and took a sip of coffee. Clint's story had taken a good part of the day, and they were now finishing up a small portion of ham and eggs.

"So you're certain that it was Willow who knocked you out?" she asked.

Clint nodded. "Yeah. It was all hazy for a while, but once my head cleared and I talked it through, I'm certain of it. Besides, she wasn't there when I woke up."

"I guess she figured the only way she could do what she wanted was to knock you over the head and take off on her own."

"She was right," Clint grumbled. "There's no way I was going to let her ride off and throw herself back into the hands of those slavers. Actually, I was planning on tying her up if she kept insisting to go."

"She's a brave woman. Perhaps she has a shot at getting her plan to work. After all, she did make it through The Gunsmith himself."

Clint gave her a humorless smile and sipped his own coffee. "Well, it's too late for me to do anything about it now. Her horse was gone and she bought herself one hell of a head start. After all the circling and backtracking we did, she only needed to be paying a little attention to know this country almost as well as I do."

"And if she's that bound and determined to go," Abby said, finishing Clint's line of thought, "then she's going to find a way to do it."

"Yeah," Clint grunted as he gently rubbed the back of his head. "I can attest to that."

Just then, there was a knock on the door. Abby stood up and walked over as the knocking became so hard that it rattled the door on its hinges. When she pulled it open, she saw the man with the pockmarked face standing there.

"What's the matter, Art?" she asked.

Art shifted so he could look past Abby and see Clint sitting at her table. Looking back at her, he said, "I think you know what I'm here for. There are some folks who still want to hang that fellow in there for killing them two men."

"How long have you lived here?"

"Huh?"

"Answer the question, Art. How long have you lived in Sharps?"

"About six months, I guess."

"And what about the ones that want to hang Clint? Are they new to town?"

Art shrugged and then nodded. "Came in from the Dakotas over the spring."

"Seems to me that they've wanted to string up anyone who looked at them funny. If you or they were here the last time Clint was in town, they'd know better than to be so quick to judge him."

"Yeah. That's what some other folks have said. They told me to come talk to you about it." Leaning in, Art lowered his voice to a whisper. "If he's hurting you, ma'am, you can tell me. I thought I heard some funny sounds a while ago."

Abby laughed, but somehow managed to keep herself from blushing. "We've been catching up on old times. Clint told me about what happened with those men. They killed each other and then Clint was knocked over the head by an Indian woman."

"Was she wearing a deerskin skirt with a white shirt?" Art asked.

"That's the one. Have you seen her?"

He nodded. "I seen her ride off after the shooting stopped."

The moment Clint heard that, he got to his feet and walked to the door. "Which way was she headed?"

"South," Art told him. "She was in an awful hurry too."

"Did anyone see the rest of those men that rode in here with that big Indian with the gold in his hair?"

"You mean the dead fella?"

"Yeah. That's the one."

Art scrunched his nose and scratched his head as he thought that over. "I believe there was one other that came into town with them two dead ones, but ain't nobody seen him for a while. Least, not as far as I know."

"Think you could look into it for me?" Abby asked.

"Sure, Abby." Abe started to turn away, but stopped and took another look at Clint. "So, he's not troubling you any?"

She shook her head. "Not a bit."

"Some of the others vouched for him, but them boys from the Dakotas wanted me to come in and see for myself. I guess he doesn't seem to be doing any harm."

"You can talk to him directly if you like, you know."

When Art glanced into the house, he got a friendly wave from Clint. He then shrugged and said, "If you back up what everyone else is saying, than I don't have a problem." Once again, he leaned in and whispered, "But if you need any help, just let us know."

"I will, Art. Thanks."

Art nodded, finally returned Clint's wave, and walked off. He stopped after a few steps and snapped his fingers. Abby was just about to close the door when he stuck his nose back through the opening. "One more thing. I almost forgot."

"What is it?" she asked.

"This just came in for Mr. Adams," he said while fishing a folded piece of paper from his pocket. "I guess since he ain't under suspicion no more, it's safe to give it to him."

She took the paper and said, "I'll see to it, thanks."

Art was midway through tipping his hat again when Abby shut the door in his face.

"You'll have to excuse them," she said. "Sometimes I think they're a little too anxious to keep thc peace around here."

"There's plenty of vigilantes in Montana," Clint said. "Just be sure your town doesn't wind up being run by them. That's not a pretty sight."

She shrugged and handed over the paper she'd been given. Rather than lecture her about her own town's policies, Clint unfolded the note and read it.

THIRTY-THREE

"Mason somehow got to a telegraph office," Clint said while reading. "He's still following the wagons and they're still headed more or less in this direction. They're camped right now about a day or two's ride from here."

"Well, that's good news, more or less."

"More or less won't cut it. At this point, it's all or nothing." After saying that, Clint stood up and started gathering his things. "Would you mind if I took some food? I've got a long ride ahead of me."

After dropping the latch on the door, Abby rushed over to Clint and pulled his saddlebags from his hand. "Where do you think you're going?"

"Weren't you listening to the whole story? I need to find Willow or catch up to those wagons."

She rushed around to stand in front of him, and had to struggle to keep him from getting away. When Clint finally did come to a stop, she pushed him back down onto one of the nearby chairs.

"You're still recovering from that head wound," she

said. "And your legs were still wobbly even when you were just trying to swing those saddlebags over your shoulder. Don't tell me you'll be able to hold onto that stallion when he gets up to a full gallop."

"I'll manage," Clint replied.

"That's not good enough. Right now, it's all or nothing, remember? All I ask is you stay off your feet for another few hours. Either those wagons are headed this way or they're not. Right now, there's no way for you to turn them and still keep to your plan. This will at least let you get the rest of your wits about you so you can decide what to do from there."

Clint started to grumble and move her aside, but Abby wouldn't budge. Instead, she started unbuttoning his shirt and peeling it off him.

"What the hell are you doing?" he asked.

"Keeping you busy for a little bit. At least long enough so you can rush out of town without those overanxious vigilantes chasing you and maybe putting a bullet in your back."

Clint let out an exasperated breath. "First of all you throw my own words back at me, and then you have the gall to make complete sense at the worst possible time."

"You sound upset," she said with a little pout. Reaching between Clint's legs, she rubbed him to a full erection through his jeans. "Funny, but it feels like you're pretty happy to me."

Rather than try to argue with her or make up an excuse about why he should go when he knew he should give it a little more time, Clint pulled Abby onto his lap and gave her a passionate kiss.

She slipped her tongue into his mouth and wriggled in his lap until she could feel the bulge of his cock rubbing against the sweet spot between her thighs. Although she eased her lips away from his, Abby kept her mouth close enough to Clint's skin that he never stopped feeling the heat from her breaths.

Abby worked her way down along Clint's chin and then to his neck, planting small, quick kisses every step of the way. Working her way down his chest, she eased off his lap and finally lowered herself onto her knees in front of him.

She looked up at him with a mischievous smile while unbuckling his belt and pulling open his jeans. Clint looked down at her, enjoying the way she watched him as her hands busily undressed him from the waist down. He especially liked the way her full, red lips parted slightly as she took hold of his rigid penis in one hand.

"It may be a long time before I see you again," she said. "I figured I should take advantage of you before you ride off."

With that, Abby slid her fingers all the way down to the base of his shaft and touched her bottom lip to the tip of his cock. Still keeping her eyes locked onto Clint's, she slipped her tongue out to glide along the bottom of his thick column of flesh. She then opened her mouth a bit wider and then slowly wrapped her lips around him.

Lowering her head between Clint's legs, Abby took almost all of him into her mouth. When she raised her head again, she moved her hand up as well to massage the part of his cock that her lips had yet to touch.

Clint felt his eyes drooping and his entire body relaxing. When she took him in her mouth again, Abby slid her lips down a bit further. Before long, Clint found himself slipping his fingers through her hair so he could brush it away from her face while also gently guiding her.

It turned out that she didn't need one bit of guidance. The next time she put her lips on him, she smiled widely and moved her hands up along his stomach. Only then did she break eye contact with him, but it was more than worth it.

Abby closed her eyes and let out a soft purr as she

wrapped her lips around his cock and took every inch of it into her mouth. Her tongue wriggled along him the entire way down, sending a shiver all the way up Clint's spine.

She could feel his hands tightening as he closed his fists around her hair. The purring sound in her throat became an aroused moan, which sent more chills through Clint as she sucked him with renewed intensity.

This time, it was Clint who struggled to keep from making too much noise. That wasn't too difficult since, every time he managed to catch his breath, Abby took it right away from him again. Her mouth was sliding along every inch of his penis, coaxing him into a powerful erection. The harder he got, the more Abby worked her tongue on him.

She could feel him getting more excited as he started shifting in his seat and grinding his hips against her mouth. Abby responded by bobbing her head up and down even faster between his legs. She had only the tip of his cock in her mouth when she started making little circles with her tongue around it.

That nearly drove Clint out of his mind, and soon he felt his climax bearing down on him. She kept right on sucking him until the last bit of his climax had worked its way through him.

Abby stood up and smiled at him. "I think you may need to stay a bit longer. You still look a little shaky."

"Come here," Clint said as he pulled her to him. "Let's see how steadily I can ride."

THIRTY-FOUR

Clint wished he could have taken that knock to the back of the head without passing out.

He wished he could have stopped Willow from leaving him at that barn, or at least talked some sense into her before she made up her mind.

He wished that Eclipse was fast enough to take him to those wagons in a few minutes.

He even wished that Mason wasn't the one who had to ride just outside of those slavers' sights to keep an eye on them without being captured or killed himself.

Clint wished plenty of things, but he knew that all the wishes under the sun didn't amount to anything when compared to the way things were. A wish couldn't stand alone, and some wishes weren't much more than smoke rings that broke apart at the slightest breeze. But even that didn't keep Clint from thinking about those wishes.

He needed something to pass the time it took for Eclipse to carry him to the spot described in Mason's telegram.

Besides the most obvious reasons, Clint was glad that

Abby had insisted that he stay with her for a little while longer. Not only did it allow him to get some more coffee in his system and clear his head a bit more, but it allowed him to be there when Art came back to give his report.

Art had been busy while Clint and Abby took some time for themselves. In fact, Art had even managed to hear a few stories concerning the third scout that they'd been after since getting into Sharps.

It seemed that that man had been asking some questions of his own concerning his two missing partners. Since nobody at Line's Emporium really knew any names to go along with the bodies in Abby's barn, the third scout got nothing for his trouble. Since he rode out in a hurry soon after he'd asked his questions, Clint could only assume that the scout had assumed the worst and gone to meet up with the slavers.

The upshot of it all was that Clint managed to catch sight of the scout not too long after leaving town. Either Abby's timing had been inspired or the fates were just with him, but Clint had been delayed just long enough for the third scout to do what he needed to do and leave.

Their paths had crossed again a few minutes ago, and Clint could only chalk it up to dumb luck. Then again, after following or avoiding the scouts for so long, Clint already felt like he knew what they were thinking before they did. Whatever the explanation, he decided not to question it.

The scout was riding so low in the saddle that his horse almost looked as if it was on its own. He kept one arm wrapped around the horse's neck and the other on his holster. Every couple of seconds, he would shoot a glance over his shoulder before using his heels to coax the horse to go faster.

Clint hung back just enough to keep the scout in his sight. More often than not, the rider wasn't much more than a speck moving in the distance. When they rode over a flat stretch of land, Clint would take a closer look using his spyglass.

The scout had a lot of talent in the saddle. More than once, he almost shook Clint off his tail. Even so, Clint managed to stay back and keep out of the scout's sight. He used the scout's speed to his advantage, creeping in closer, knowing full well that no one could see everything when he was taking glances over his shoulder while riding like he had the devil on his heels.

Before too long, Clint could see what the scout had in mind. Just like they'd done when all the scouts had been together and riding as a group, the lone scout was inching in one direction before making a clean break in another.

Clint could feel the scout getting ready to make the turn, which would point him toward where Mason's telegram had said the wagons were waiting. Sure enough, when the sun was just about to set, the scout turned toward the blazing light of dusk and dug his heels into horseflesh.

Of course, by this time, Clint had already steered Eclipse in that same direction and had already managed to close the gap between himself and that scout.

The Darley Arabian tore over the ground like a bullet, his powerful head chugging like a steam engine's piston. Clint hung on for dear life, grinning from ear to ear as he tried to keep watch on the scout through the swirling dust and setting sun.

He couldn't let that scout get back to the wagons.

Clint had decided that soon after leaving Sharps.

If that scout made it back alone, he would tell the slavers what had happened to the others and nothing good could come out of that. If Willow had made it to the wagons, she would be tortured even further for information. And if she told what happened to Avery and Ka'lanu, she would probably be killed as some twisted form of vengeance.

At the very least, Umberto wouldn't be too anxious to

take any suggestions concerning the direction of his wagons. Willow was right about one thing: They'd come too far to give up on the plan now. While she felt she owed it to her brother to go through with it, Clint figured he owed it to her to do the same.

It had been a long road and along the way, Clint's plan had been blown to hell more than once. Therefore, he decided to keep his head down and take each step the moment he decided where to plant his foot. That was how he wound up speeding through Montana, preparing to overtake a rider whose finger was already itching to pull a trigger.

Now it was Clint's turn to ride low against Eclipse's neck. He moved like he was a part of the Darley Arabian simply because it was either that or be tossed off like an old shirt. After a slight detour to swing around and turn back again, Clint managed to cut in front of the scout's path.

When the scout saw Clint coming, it was too late for him to do anything about it.

By the time the scout thought to draw his pistol, Clint had already cleared leather.

In a matter of moments, Eclipse was off and running.

There was nobody willing or able to follow.

THIRTY-FIVE

It was first light and the wagon master was making his rounds and rousing anybody who wasn't already on his feet. He kicked men in their ribs or even tossed a few from where they'd been sleeping as the rest of the camp around him came to life.

"Rise and shine in there," he said while knocking on one of the prisoners' wagons. "We got another long ride ahead of us. Don't worry, though, because you'll all find some new homes soon enough." As he walked away, he didn't try to hide the cruel laugh that accompanied the thought of those prisoners' future.

Inside that wagon, nobody had been able to sleep. Their bodies were cramped too close together and the nightmare was too close to the surface for them to dare close their eyes.

Just as the wagon master's steps were fading, another set of heavier boots slapped against the ground on their way to the wagon. The familiar sound of labored breathing made all the prisoners press themselves as far back into the wagon as they could. Even if the wagon was twice as big, however, they wouldn't be able to get far enough away from that door as it was pulled open.

To the prisoners inside the wagon, the daylight streaming through the doorway was almost blinding. All of them recoiled instinctively when they saw the glare, but started to move toward it when they felt its warmth. That latter impulse died as soon as they saw the ugly face peering in at them.

Straining to get a look into the wagon, Umberto scowled widely enough for his gold tooth to catch some of the light. "Where's my girl?" he wheezed.

Reaching in with a dirty hand, Umberto shoved aside a few of the other prisoners as if he was picking one puppy out of a litter. He swatted away a few hands, but soon wrapped his fingers around the arm he was after. Grinning with his little victory caused the drooping ends of his long mustache to waggle.

"There you are, *chiquita*. I missed you."

Willow could barely open her eyes. She'd only managed to fall asleep a few minutes ago and that was only because she was too tired to stand. Even as she was pulled out of the wagon, she was too dazed to fight. She'd had so many nightmares exactly like this that she wasn't certain this was actually happening.

After pulling Willow from the wagon, Umberto slammed the door shut and stepped aside so one of his men could lock it. He dragged Willow by a section of her shirt as if he was carrying a cat by the scruff of its neck. He took her to another wagon, which was already open, and tossed her in.

When Umberto climbed into the wagon, it creaked and tilted under his weight. "So," he said while settling onto a small stool. "I'd like to hear where you've been these last few weeks."

Willow could only look at the fat Mexican for a few moments before averting her eyes.

Reaching out to take hold of her chin, Umberto forced her to look at him again. "I asked you a question, *chiquita.* I take care of you all this time and you repay me by running away?" When Willow tried to look away again, he slapped her viciously across the face.

Since he kept hold of her chin, the impact of his hand rattled her right down to the bone. She felt dizzy after that one hit, and, by the look in his eyes, there were plenty more to come.

"I don't like to hurt my girls," Umberto said. "But you don't leave me much choice. Tell me how you got loose and where you went, or I'll have to hurt you some more."

Willow tried to shake her head, but couldn't get free of Umberto's grasp. Even trying to speak was a chore since his fingers were practically holding her mouth shut.

"No," she said. "I'll tell you noth—"

She was cut off by another quick slap. Umberto let go of her face, but that was only so he could send a sharp jab into her chin.

Willow had never been hit with such deliberate brutality before. She'd been in a few scuffles as a child and was treated roughly when she was first captured, but it was nothing like this. Umberto's only purpose was to hurt her, and he was very good at it.

With those three blows, Willow could feel her face starting to swell and jolts of pain coming in from all sides. It hurt to breathe. It even hurt to blink.

"I've just started with you, *chiquita.* You want to play some more?"

She shook her head weakly.

"Then tell me how you got out."

"When . . . they brought the food," she groaned. "The door was open and I . . . slipped out."

Umberto nodded. In the few seconds that passed, every movement he made seemed like it was going to lead to another punch or slap. Finally, he leaned back to give Willow some space.

"All right," he said. "Go on."

"The others told me not to . . . but I ran away."

"And where did you go?"

"I ran . . . west."

"You ran the whole way?" Umberto asked. "This whole time?"

Willow dropped her head and tried to think about something other than the way her lip was swelling to double its original size. Before she could take two steady breaths in a row, she heard Umberto grunt as he shifted his weight and then felt his meaty fist slam into the side of her head.

Brilliant flashes sparked in her field of vision and her eyesight began to blur. Willow didn't have a chance to cover herself before another punch landed between her shoulder and the base of her neck. His fist dropped like an iron weight and sent her flat to the floor.

"You don't stop talking until I tell you," Umberto said as Willow clawed at the floor of the wagon. "Next time you make me ask you, I'll use this on you."

She wasn't able to lift her head, but Willow recognized the sound a knife made as it was pulled from its scabbard.

THIRTY-SIX

Mason had never been so filthy for so long in his life. Any man who rode the trails and camped for weeks at a time knew what it was like to be dirty, but that was why God created streams and waterfalls. This time, however, no matter how many pools of water Mason saw, he was forced to keep away from every last one of them.

The wagons had been rolling from one source of water to the next. They set up camp at the best spots, since those were obviously what they used as reference points when working their way north. Mason learned that much fairly soon after he'd started following them.

Of course, the problem was that he couldn't get to that water himself without getting too close to the wagons and the armed men guarding them. He could barely slip past the scouts long enough to refill his canteens every now and then.

By this point, every inch of Mason's face was caked in dirt and grime. His teeth were like moss-covered rocks at the bottom of a stream and his clothes practically stuck to him.

The only saving grace was that Mason had been in this state for long enough that he'd somehow gotten used to it. He didn't even bother propping himself up anymore when he was lying in the dirt to watch the wagons from afar. Sleeping without a campfire had become second nature, and his ears were so attuned to the noises around him that he could damn near identify each individual cricket by the angle it used when rubbing its legs together.

When he heard the rustle of nearby footsteps, he froze in his spot and took his knife in hand. After that, he held his breath and waited for another sound.

The steps stopped less than a few feet from where Mason was stretched out on the ground. He could tell by the easy way the man breathed that he probably didn't know he was being watched. Gritting his teeth and tensing his muscles, Mason pulled his legs beneath him and pounced.

Clint had just enough time to turn and catch the man who was flying at him like a crazed trap-door spider. He managed to get one hand out to protect himself while his other hand plucked the modified Colt from its holster.

Clint twisted at the waist and sent the filthy man to the ground.

Mason had already braced himself for impact, and was ready to swipe across the other man's throat with his blade.

After a few seconds, both men realized who they were facing.

"Clint?" Mason gasped. "Is that you?"

"Yeah," Clint replied without lowering the Colt. "It's me."

"You got my telegram?"

For a moment, Clint didn't respond. He was too busy taking in the sight of Mason's dirt-covered face. Finally, he managed to decipher enough of Mason's features to truly recognize the bounty hunter.

"I got it," Clint said. "I just wish I could have been there to see you send it. You look like you've been sleeping under a log since I left you."

"It was rough at first, but I got used to it."

Clint recoiled and fanned the air in front of him. "How long will it take for me to get used to that smell?"

"A couple of weeks. Now get down before you're spotted. These scouts know their business."

Clint hunkered down next to the bounty hunter. They were inside a cluster of trees at the base of a wide range of tall rocks. A small crevice cut through the rocks behind them, but was covered by a thick clump of bushes. The trees were scattered here and there in front of the rocks, covering several other winding paths that led to anything from small trails to dead ends.

Less than half a mile in front of them was a trail that Clint knew very well. It was used by travelers and traders alike, but had fallen into disuse after robbers had killed a dozen men and stole over twenty thousand dollars over the course of six months.

"I think that's more use than that road has seen in a while," Clint said.

Mason nodded. "That's how they travel. If I didn't know any better, I'd admire the bastards. They move right under everyone's noses and most of the time, they're right out in front of other folks and even the law."

"They've slipped past the law?"

"Slipped past don't exactly cover it. Rolled right past is more like it. I've seen the wagon master stop to have a chat with deputies and even a marshal or two before everyone parted ways like they was old friends. Of course, from where I was, I could tell the men in some of them wagons was ready to blow those lawmen to hell if things took a wrong turn."

"Was anyone hurt?"

"Nope. Never any need for it. I think these slavers got their route so well worn that they're recognized by half the folks they see. The other half doesn't even think to make them out to be anything else besides just another wagon train."

"Did you see Willow?"

Mason nodded as he placed his spyglass to his eye. "She came back yesterday. When I saw her, I figured you must have been hurt or killed. What happened?"

"It's a long story. The short of it is that she took off on her own to try and do the jobs we were hoping her brother could do."

"Is that Injun dead?"

"Yeah."

"Shame," Mason grunted. "He could've done some good. But we can work without him. Those wagons have already started to turn toward that town of yours."

"What?" Clint said as he quickly crawled forward so he could get a look at the wagons.

Taking in the view from that vantage point allowed him to see almost the entire group. Sure enough, the front of the line was bending to the east.

"I'll be damned," Clint whispered. "Whatever she had in mind must have worked."

"Looks like it. I'd say we've got another couple of days before those wagons hit that canyon. That is, if they decide to take that trail."

"They won't have any choice. It's the only one big enough to accommodate all those wagons, remember?"

"I guess," Mason said. "So far, I haven't seen them be driven onto any trail that forced them to go single file. They tend to prefer routes where they can bunch up or turn around if need be."

"Let's keep our fingers crossed. Now we should think about a way to get those prisoners' wagons separated from the pack. I doubt Willow will have any way to make that happen."

"Oh, I've already been working on that," Mason replied casually.

Clint looked over at the bounty hunter. "And what have you come up with?"

"Not a plan half as complicated as yours, but it seems to be working just fine. All I needed to do was slow the horses down that pull those carts. Them slavers tend to keep the same animals pulling the same loads. At least, I've never seen them switch any out unless they was injured."

Clint was still looking at Mason with a bit of disbelief. "You've already started this?"

"Sure. Why else have I been out here in the elements all this time? I've been sneaking into that camp every night since you left. All I need to do is stick a few pebbles under a few horseshoes and tamper with a few wheels and those wagons will drift right to the back on their own."

Clint took another look at the wagons through his spyglass as Mason kept talking.

"I found that doctoring a mule's water does wonders, but it doesn't last long," the bounty hunter explained. "I've slowed down more than one outlaw that way. Nothing's better to cut a getaway real short."

"I'll be damned," Clint said. "Are those two wagons at the back full of prisoners?"

"Sure are. They still don't know why the horses don't feel like working as hard as the others." Mason shook his head and smirked. "Them assholes may know how to run prisoners across state lines, but they sure are piss-poor cowboys."

"What about the rest of the prisoners?"

"Near as I can tell, there's only one other wagon, and that's been kept closer to the front because it's where they're holding that squaw friend of yours."

"Willow? Where is she?"

Mason pointed out the wagon, but Clint couldn't see anything happening there at the moment.

"All right then," Clint said. "Looks like we've got our work cut out for us. What about the scouts escorting those wagons? Where are they?"

Mason craned his neck to look at the rocks towering above and behind them.

"You've got to be joking," Clint whispered.

Mason smirked wide enough to crack the mud on his face. "Exciting, ain't it?"

THIRTY-SEVEN

The wagons rolled through Sharps without stopping for more than a few hours. That was enough time for the slavers to water the horses and send in a few carts to bring back supplies to the rest of the caravan. Clint and Mason stuck together during this time, which was enough for Clint to pick up on Mason's habits.

Although Clint wouldn't admit it to the bounty hunter directly, he even learned a few things in that time.

Mostly, Clint learned how to hide in plain sight. Mason made it a habit to keep just within the scouts' range. Since the escort riders tended to stick to the higher ground, keeping close and in front of them was similar to hiding right beneath a window. Anyone looking in your direction would look straight over your head.

The canyon that Clint had drawn countless times loomed in front of them to the northeast. Although it wasn't too impressive from where they were, Clint knew the trail dipped down low in several spots, which would be the spots where he would launch his attack. The more he thought about that attack, however, the more he started to question it.

"I must be crazy," Clint muttered.

He and Mason were sitting in their saddles, watching the wagons roll down the very trail that would take them into the canyon. The wagons had already taken on another formation as if to remind Clint just how many guns the slavers were carrying.

"Hell, Adams," Mason grunted. "I been thinking that ever since you hatched this plan."

"Why didn't you say something?"

"I did! You're just too damn stubborn to change your mind." Reaching out to pat Clint on the shoulder, Mason added, "But you're the only man I know who could have pulled it off. Look at that caravan. It's rolling right where you wanted it to go."

"We got lucky."

"Luck don't mean shit. What means anything is that we bit off more than we could chew, and we just kept on chewing until we ate the whole damn thing."

Clint looked over at the bounty hunter and had to laugh. "What in the hell does that mean?"

"I'm trying to pay you a compliment."

"I think you've been sleeping in the mud too long. Some of it's leaked into your brain."

"I'm actually starting to think we might be able to pull this off. And that ain't the mud talking."

Clint shook his head and kept his eyes on the rolling wagons. "Willow's down there right where she started. For all I know, she could be hurt or dead right now."

"That's her doing. She broke away from you, remember?"

"Her brother's dead and that's because I got involved."

"I wasn't there, but it sounds like that wasn't your fault."

"And after all of that, there's still a big chance that this won't even work."

"Take a look around, Adams. There's been fewer and

fewer scouts swarming around them wagons with each passing day. That's our doing. That squaw and her brother took a stand against them slavers because they knew it was the right thing. That was your doing as well and you'd be a damn fool to be ashamed of it.

"Somehow, we managed to steer those wagons here, so there ain't no reason why the rest of this plan can't work out. Besides, don't you think it's a little late to be grousing about all of this now?"

Clint shrugged. "I guess I haven't had enough time to think about all of it until now."

"Or maybe it's been a while since you've been able to go anywhere without looking over your shoulder or worrying about keeping dozens of people alive. This has been playing hell with you just like it has on everyone else, Adams. Believe it or not, I've had my moments of doubt along the way."

"So you really want to go through with this?" Clint asked.

Mason shrugged and replied, "Too late to back out now."

Clint looked further up the trail using his spyglass. It was just as he remembered it and there were no other trails branching out to lead around the canyon. In fact, some of the scouts were already splitting off to ride up to the higher ground.

When he looked back, he saw the wagons beginning to move into a two-by-two formation. Most of the prisoners were still at the back of the caravan.

"Are you really ready for this?" Clint asked. "I don't want you to go through with this unless—"

"Hey, I'm the one that asked you along for this ride, remember?"

"All right then. Let's see it through."

THIRTY-EIGHT

The scouts rode in pairs as they climbed to the top of the rocks and surveyed the canyon. It wasn't the first time they'd seen the formation, but it had been a while since they'd taken that particular route. After the way things had been going, none of the scouts were too happy with this new change in direction.

"Where the hell are they?" the first scout asked while searching the rocks on the other side of the canyon.

The second scout had ridden a little ways ahead and now came up alongside his partner. "You want to know what I think?"

"If I did, I would'a said so."

"I think Avery and them others got drunk and landed themselves in jail. Or maybe it was that Injun that got them in trouble. You know Injuns can't handle their liquor."

"They ain't the ones I was talking about."

"Or maybe they're still with some whores over in Sharps. Remember the last time we was in Sharps? Them whores could suck the—"

"Shut your mouth!" the first scout snapped. "And open yer goddamn eyes like yer paid to do."

"What the hell's your problem?"

Rather than say another word, the first scout reached out to grab hold of the second one's ear. He pulled the younger man like he was taking a child to the woodshed and then shoved his face forward. "Look out there and tell me what you see!"

The second scout tried to swat away the other's hand, but wound up having to tear himself away and lose some skin to get free. "I don't see anything!"

"Right. Now, shouldn't Abe and Jacob be over there getting into position?"

"Yeah."

"Then where are they?"

The second scout swiped away the blood from his ear and wiped it on his shirt. Riding his horse right to the edge of the rock, he leaned forward in his saddle and squinted toward the other side. Finally, he said, "Where the hell are they?"

Letting out a sigh that sounded more like steam coming from a kettle, the first scout gritted his teeth. "Ride along this ridge and see if you can spot them. I'll wait here in case they come back."

Grumbling to himself, the second scout snapped his reins and rode along the top of the ridge. The trees grew into a thick tangle the further along he went, stretching overhead until most of the sunlight was blocked. Toward the end of the ridge, a chunk of rock jutted upward about eight or nine feet; covered with vines and moss.

Pausing in the cool shade, the scout squinted across the canyon and shook his head. "They ain't there," he shouted.

When he didn't hear a response, he took another few steps forward and shaded his eyes once he left the shade. Feeling the heat almost immediately, he backed his horse into the cooler area.

"Anything yet?" came the first scout's voice.

"I don't see anyone."

Since he didn't budge from where he was standing, he obviously didn't see the shape that peeled itself away from the rock wall behind him.

Mason had vines draped over his shoulders and dirt smeared even thicker onto his face. In the shadows provided by the trees, he looked like a piece of swampland that had sprouted eyes and legs.

"Lazy bastard," the scout muttered as he reached into his shirt pocket for some tobacco. "Next time he can do all the extra riding."

Mason reached out with both hands and pulled the scout from his saddle. Before the scout could let out one word or even yelp in surprise, Mason had punched him in the face three times. A few twitches followed by an exhale, and the scout was done.

Just to be certain, Mason buried the blade of his knife under the scout's chin and twisted.

"What the hell's keeping ya?" shouted the first scout.

"Goddamn it," the first scout mumbled as he shifted in his saddle.

He strained his eyes, but could only make out the back end of the other man's horse. Leaning forward and straining some more only allowed him to catch a glimpse of the saddle.

"You see anyone across the way yet?"

No answer.

"If you're taking a piss, I'll come over there and cut yer damn pecker off!"

Still nothing.

As the scout shifted his eyes from the part of the horse he could see to the ridge on the other side of the canyon, he started to get uneasy. The moment he felt that, he shut his mouth and strained to hear anything out of the ordinary.

The scout's hand drifted to the rifle stored on the side of his saddle, but only touched against bare leather.

"What the—"

Before the scout could make another sound, he saw a man covered in vines and dirt stand up and stretch out one arm. He could feel the rifle barrel pressing against his ribs.

Mason pulled the trigger and the rifle went off with a muffled thump.

A red mist exploded out the scout's back and his jaw dropped open.

Reaching out with his free hand, Mason took hold of the scout's arm and pulled him off his horse. The animal hadn't even heard enough to be spooked. The scout landed heavily on the ground, where his throat was immediately cut.

Mason glanced across the canyon and let out a whistle. When he saw Clint stick his head up, he gave him a wave. He got the same wave in return, letting him know that the top of the canyon was now clear.

Both men just hoped the rest of the plan went that smoothly.

THIRTY-NINE

Clint waved across the canyon and soon saw Mason wave back. Although he didn't have much question that his half of the rocks was clear, Clint took one more look over his shoulder to where he'd left the pair of scouts that had been there. Sure enough, they were still knocked out, had their arms and legs tied, and wouldn't be found until the smoke had cleared.

For some reason, Clint had the feeling that the scouts on Mason's side of the canyon weren't so lucky.

Lowering himself onto his belly, Clint inched his way to the edge of the rock ledge so he could take a look at what was happening down below. The wagons were still moving slowly and settling into their new formation. He looked through his spyglass to find most of the wagons' drivers were shifting restlessly in their seats.

"Good," Clint thought. "Just sit back and be bored with the ride. That'll make things nice and easy."

He and Mason had gone over the rest of the plan several times as they'd crept their way up to the top of the canyon.

Even when Clint had been knocking out and tying up the scouts he'd found, he'd still been going over the details in his head. He knew all too well that things rarely went according to any man's plan, but he wasn't about to be caught without one.

He gazed through the spyglass to study the wagons rolling beneath him. Mason had told him how to recognize the ones carrying the prisoners, and it did seem that those were rattling toward the back of the line. Their wheels were wobbly and the horses pulling them looked tired.

The liquor Mason had slipped into their water the night before still seemed to be having an effect. Part of Clint wondered what the hell else was in Mason's flask besides whiskey. The other part of him didn't even want to know.

What mattered was the fact that only one prisoner wagon wasn't in the back of the line, and that one was toward the middle. The wagons at the front of the caravan were rolling past Clint's position and moving slower by the second.

Shifting his attention to the front of the line, Clint could see the men in the front wagons' seats looking up at the top of the ridge. The more they studied those rocks, the more confused they looked. Then, as one of them motioned with a few waves of his arm, the wagons started slowing even more.

Clint pressed himself against the rock and scooted away from the ledge. Lifting only his eyes, he found the barely noticeable bump across from him that was Mason keeping himself equally hidden.

The two men looked at each other across the canyon using their spyglasses. That was the only way Mason was able to see the subtle hand gestures given by Clint. Mason replied with a few gestures of his own, making certain to keep his hands, head, and everything else low enough to remain hidden from the wagons below.

Once the signals were through, Mason eased a rifle to

his shoulder and Clint shimmied his way down the back of the rock face.

"Whoa there," the wagon master said as he waved. Standing up in his seat, he lifted both arms and waved them vigorously over his head. Soon, he heard his command being echoed by the other drivers behind him.

Like clockwork, Umberto rode up next to the lead wagon. "What's the holdup?" he asked.

"I can't see the scouts," the wagon master replied.

Umberto craned his neck to look upward, and winced as sunlight turned his field of vision into a washed-out mess of white and yellow. "I can't see anything up there."

"We sent the scouts to watch over us a while ago. They should be there."

"Maybe they couldn't find a quick path up to the top. Or maybe they've already moved on."

"I saw them up there before."

"Then what's the problem?"

"They should still be up there! That's the problem." Taking a breath and stopping himself before saying something he would regret, the wagon master forced a more respectful tone in his voice when he continued. "You and I both know that there should at least be two of those scouts in sight at all times. Since they were there a few minutes ago, then something must have happened for them to be gone now."

Although Umberto wasn't known to tolerate anyone speaking to him with a sharp tone, he merely nodded at the wagon master. "You're right. I just don't like being stopped right here."

"There's not enough room to turn around," the wagon master said after taking a quick look at the trail. "But we should be able to back out."

Clint was halfway down the rocks, hunkered down in his saddle. The trail he'd taken to the top was the same one the scouts had used. It was narrow and almost completely covered by trees and thick bushes, which became thicker the closer they got to the bottom. Right now, Clint was at the last spot Eclipse could go before rustling leaves and snapping branches announced his every movement.

He couldn't see much more than a few wheels of two lead wagons. The wagons themselves had stopped.

"Come on," he whispered under his breath. "Just a little farther."

Umberto's face twisted into an unhappy frown before he shook his head. "We'll take it slow, but there's no sense in turning back. We've added enough time on this already and heading back will only bring us closer to those marshals."

"But if something's happened to the scouts, that could mean—"

"Do what I tell you to do," Umberto snarled. "We've got enough firepower to blast a hole through these goddamn rocks. We can make it through this goddamn canyon!"

Grudgingly, the wagon master snapped his reins and motioned for the caravan to roll forward.

FORTY

The wagons moved on amid the sounds of creaking wheels, snapping leather, and winded horses. As they rolled past the spot where Clint was waiting, he smiled and prepared himself for the next step in his plan.

Once the third row of wagons moved past him, Clint snapped his reins and got Eclipse racing down the trail. As the Darley Arabian crashed through the low-hanging branches and stomped over layers of fallen leaves and twigs, Clint thought about all the details that had led up to this moment.

The only one that truly mattered was the wagon that Mason had pointed out to him earlier. It was a wagon that he knew to be loaded with guns and ammunition. When he'd shown it to Clint, the wagon looked a lot like the one that Clint had inspected himself during his first visit to the camp.

But the time for planning, watching, and waiting were over.

Now was the time to act, and it was too late to turn back.

Eclipse exploded from the cover of branches like he'd been shot from a cannon. The stallion's eyes were wild and he trusted his rider enough to charge forward no matter what was in front of him. He didn't flinch when he saw the wagons less than two yards from the side of the trail. Instead, he waited for Clint's command before turning hard and running alongside the covered cart.

Clint heard men shouting in surprise and barking orders, but the blood rushing through his ears combined with the thunder of Eclipse's hooves was more than enough to wash those sounds away.

Now that he was clear of the branches and Eclipse was running on less cluttered ground, Clint could hear the sounds of all hell breaking loose around him.

"Who the hell is that?" someone shouted.

". . . not one of ours . . ."

But one of the voices could be heard above all the others as it roared, "Shoot him!"

Gunshots began cracking through the air and lead whipped over Clint's head. A few rounds hissed to his left, but most of the men firing were doing their best to keep from hitting the wagon. That meant so far, everything was going according to plan.

Clint pulled a knife from its scabbard and used it to slice open the tarp covering the wagon. With his other hand, he pulled back on Eclipse's reins to keep the stallion from racing past the wagon altogether. Eclipse had enough speed to drag Clint's knife through the wagon's tarp, and slowed down just as Clint reached the two surprised drivers up front.

The man closest to Clint had a shotgun in hand and was taking aim when the weapon was suddenly yanked from his grasp. Clint took hold of the shotgun midway down the barrel, twisted it out of the driver's fingers, and pulled it away. He then sent the stock straight into the driver's face, where it landed with a jarring crack.

While the closer of the two drivers was still wobbling in his seat, Clint got the shotgun in a proper grip and turned it on the second driver. That man was taking up a rifle when he was caught in Clint's sights. The moment he felt the shotgun's barrel jabbing into his ribs, the driver threw up both arms.

Clint didn't have time to give orders or issue demands, so he kept on pushing the shotgun into the driver's ribs until the man was forced out of his seat. After shoving the driver off the wagon completely, Clint tossed the first driver out as well and then climbed into the seat.

"I said shoot that son of a bitch!" Umberto roared.

Those words weren't even out of Umberto's mouth when the men in the wagon next to Clint's tried to carry them out. There were two in that wagon as well. One of them fired a quick shot that hissed over Clint's head, and the other was about to pull his trigger when another shot coming from above punched a hole through the top of his head.

Clint heard the shot and saw the blood spray from the driver's mouth. Since he knew where to look, he also saw the puff of smoke come from Mason's rifle at the top of the canyon. Another shot cracked through the air, to rip out a chunk of the remaining driver's shoulder just below his neck. It wasn't a mortal wound, but it took that man out of the fight.

Although he wasn't being shot at for the moment, Clint was more concerned about another matter that had just reared its head. The horses pulling the wagon had been startled by Clint's sudden appearance, but the gunshots that followed had driven them into a frenzy.

Already exhausted and hot from the long haul, the horses pulling those two wagons let out panicked whinnies and stomped their hooves against the ground. Once they regained their footing, they bolted forward to nudge the wagons in front of them.

Once the horses pulling those wagons felt that bump, they were pushed over the edge as well. Soon, the entire front portion of the caravan was charging through that canyon as if the devil himself was chasing them. More men shot in Clint's direction whether they could see him or not, spreading the chaos like a bad case of the pox.

From his perch above it all, Mason watched the show with a grin on his face. All the while, he took shot after shot with his rifle before reaching to his pouch for fresh rounds. A few of the shots had knocked out more gunmen trying to draw a bead on Clint. A few more had been aimed at the horses just to get them to kick up a bit more dust.

A group of riders was racing up from the back of the line with their guns drawn, but holding their fire until they spotted their target. Mason knew those were the men Clint needed to worry about, and quickly shoved in the last few rounds into his rifle.

The mounted gunmen were coming up the middle of the row and were only a few wagons behind Clint. Quickly levering in a fresh round, Mason sighted down the barrel of his rifle, let out a breath, and squeezed off two shots just as the first rider was about to fire a shot at Clint.

Two riders were knocked from their saddles, and Mason quickly looked for another target.

"Hot damn, Adams," Mason said under his breath. "Now this is what I call a plan."

FORTY-ONE

Clint ducked his head and kept hold of his reins. Some of the gunfire was getting uncomfortably close to its mark, and was creeping in closer by the second. Since the vicinity immediately around him was at the eye of the storm for the moment, he took advantage of the relative calm and climbed into the back of the wagon.

Sure enough, the cart was filled with munitions of all kinds. It might not have been the exact wagon he'd seen the first time he'd snuck into the camp, but it was close enough. It had all the stacks of explosives, firearms, and ammunition that he recalled, right down to the Gatling gun at the rear.

Working his way toward the Gatling gun, Clint knocked over a few of the smaller boxes until he found what he'd been looking for. When that box tipped over, several sticks of dynamite spilled out onto the floor. Trying not to think of all the possible ways he could blow himself to kingdom come, Clint filled his jacket pockets with dynamite and settled in behind the Gatling.

Rounds for the Gatling were next to the gun, right where they should be if that gun was meant for use. Clint fed the first few rounds into the gun, and then reached out to take hold of the tarp covering the back of the wagon. After pulling open the tarp, Clint rushed back to sit on his makeshift seat behind the big gun.

"Holy shit!" a rider yelled when he saw the back of that wagon come open.

The rider was one of three more who had been working their way up to Clint. They'd been caught at just the wrong time and suddenly found themselves in the middle of a shooting gallery.

Clint turned the Gatling's crank to spit out round after round of hot lead. The Gatling's barrels turned as fire blasted toward the gunmen behind the wagon, knocking those men from their saddles like the clay pigeons they were. Once those men were gone, Clint turned the Gatling toward the wagons directly behind him.

All it took was a few shots in their direction for all four drivers of those wagons to jump from their seats as quickly as their legs would carry them. The Gatling sheared off the top part of the wagons before Clint stopped turning the crank.

"All right," Clint said to himself. "Let's bring this parade to a stop."

With that, Clint adjusted his aim to the center of one of the wagons. The horses pulling both of those wagons were already bucking and rearing in their haste to get the hell away from there. Clint did his best to aim over them before turning the Gatling's crank once more. Another wave of thunder erupted from the Gatling, which punched a hole straight through the driver's seat and into the back.

One of the horses lost a bit of an ear as it tried to rear up on its hind legs, but that only served to force its head down even lower. Now that Clint had a clear shot, he lowered his aim and finally saw the results he'd been waiting for.

The next few rounds splintered wooden crates and smaller boxes. After that, the Gatling's bullets were tearing straight into the guns and ammunition stored in that wagon. All it took was one spark to ignite one box and soon the entire wagon was exploding over and over again.

Clint didn't even bother shooting into the wagon beside the one that was on fire. He knew all too well that it would go up soon enough just because it was so close to its neighbor.

By this time, the horses were whipped into such a frenzy that they'd practically busted through whatever was hitching them to their wagons. The few hitches that held were quickly weakened when a chunk of the wagon was blasted off thanks to the dynamite stored in there.

One of the horses didn't make it, but the other three were either lucky or tough enough to shake off a few flesh wounds just so they could bolt from the hellfire behind them. As soon as those three horses charged toward the front of the caravan, the remaining horses found even more incentive to do the same.

Unfortunately, the horses pulling Clint's wagon were just as spooked as the rest. When they tried to pull free of their hitches, Clint was nearly chucked right out the back of the wagon. He steadied himself as best he could, and almost made it back to the driver's seat before they lurched again.

One of the horses broke free, which splintered the wagon enough to allow the other one to bolt right after it. Clint pulled the brake just in time to hear the thunder of approaching hooves drawing up from the back of the caravan.

And just when he thought things couldn't get worse, Clint heard Umberto shouting, "Aim half of them guns at the top of that ridge. Cover the whole damn thing with lead. Aim the rest at that wagon. Whoever these bastards are, blow them all to hell!"

FORTY-TWO

Clint jumped down from the seat and ran straight for the closest wagon he could find that still had a horse attached to it. After cutting its hitches, he dug some dynamite out from his pocket along with a few matches.

Striking a match along the side of one wagon, he touched the flame to a wick and then used that wick to light two more. He tossed one stick of dynamite toward the wagons in front of him and pitched another into the wagon he'd just left.

Clint stood between the wagons, enshrouded in the black, gritty fog of burnt gunpowder. One hand was hovering over his pistol and the other was behind his back.

Umberto sat upon his horse with an Army-model revolver in one hand and his reins in the other. Judging by the look on his face, he was so surprised to see Clint step forward that he didn't quite know how to react.

"You men have one chance to give up now and take your chances with the law," Clint shouted.

Umberto's face was smeared with sweat and grime. The smirk on his face came more from bewilderment than anything else. "Or else what, gringo?"

"Or you'll have to take your chances with me."

Shaking his head, Umberto lowered his pistol to aim at Clint while he shouted, "Kill the guns up on that ridge and then kill this stupid asshole!"

"I knew you'd say that," Clint muttered. With that, Clint snapped both arms out and forward. One arm drew his modified Colt and the other tossed the stick of dynamite at one of the wagons that had been turned with its back end pointed at Mason's ridge.

Just then, the first explosion sent a deafening blast through the canyon as one of the wagons at the front of the caravan was blown to bits. Clint fired a shot at Umberto while dropping down and rolling to the side of the path as the next wagon went up in a roaring blast.

The third stick of dynamite went off, but blasted apart mostly the front section of that wagon. Since it had already lost its horses to panic, the only thing the dynamite accomplished was to loosen the brake. The wagon rolled a bit and had caught fire, but that didn't stop the Gatling gun in the back from sending a wave of hot lead up to where Mason was perched.

Clint forgot about everything else around him as he saw the top of those rocks get torn apart by not one, but two Gatlings. They tore apart everything up there from trees to rocks and anything in between. Within seconds, more guns were added to the mix, until finally Clint saw a few small objects get tossed through the air.

The dynamite exploded like thunder over Clint's head. When the guns were focused on the other side of the rocks, Clint's eyes were still glued to the spot where Mason had been.

A shot sent a round hissing past Clint, which was more than enough to snap his attention back to his immediate surroundings. Although there were plenty of men scurrying from one spot to another, a lot of them were trying to wrangle one of the frenzied horses so they could take off in any direction that would take them away from the caravan.

Umberto wasn't one of those men. Instead, he managed to keep his horse fairly calm as he headed straight toward Clint. "If you're waiting for those marshals to show up, you're in for a disappointment. We put them behind us already."

Clint wasn't exactly sure what Umberto was talking about, but he had a sneaking suspicion.

"There's plenty more where those came from," Clint said. "And they're heading straight for you. They're coming for all of you!"

Those last words echoed through the canyon, just as Clint had intended.

Umberto's eyes went up to the top of the rocks as an ugly scowl covered his face. "Either way, you won't be alive to see it, gringo." With that, Umberto took quick aim and pulled his trigger.

Clint could see the shot coming from a mile away and had already jumped for cover before it went off. Even so, Umberto's bullet came awfully close to the mark as it hissed angrily past Clint's head. The moment he got behind a smoking chunk of wagon, Clint turned and peeked around to find his target.

But Umberto was already gone. Between the several small fires, protesting horses, and shouting slavers, Clint could barely hear himself think. So rather than try to sort through the mess in his ears, he blocked it all out and concentrated on only what he could see.

Unfortunately, that was a smoky mess as well.

When Clint tried to step around the wagon he'd been using as cover, several shots were fired at him. He peered between the spokes of a broken wagon wheel and spotted two gunmen crouched behind the carcass of an unlucky horse.

Further down the caravan, more shots were being fired and smaller explosions were going off. Since the fire was spreading throughout all the wagons, it was impossible for Clint to tell which shots were intentional and which were just being set off by an ammunition box that was close to too much heat. Either way, the shots were an excellent source of cover as Clint worked his way closer to those two gunmen.

Another pop went off in the distance, causing one of the gunmen to twitch reflexively in that direction. When he turned back, he found Clint standing less than ten feet away from him.

The other gunman had already moved his gun to aim at Clint when a bullet from the modified Colt burned him down.

Clint waited to see if the remaining gunman would do the smart thing and toss his weapon, but the man decided to try where his partner had failed. The gunman lifted his gun and tightened his finger around his trigger when Clint's Colt barked again and punched a hole through his chest.

Umberto was hiding somewhere nearby. Clint could feel it in his bones. The real trick would be to see if he could find the slaver before Umberto made his way back to those prisoners.

FORTY-THREE

Willow wanted to find the darkest corner of the wagon, curl up in it, and never come out. It sounded as if the world outside was coming to an end and there wasn't anything she could do about it. But rather than give in to those thoughts, she stayed closest to the wagon's door so the rest of the prisoners could feel safer behind her.

"What's going on out there?" one of the younger girls asked.

Willow was trying to look between the boards nailed over the window, but could only see glimpses of movement. "They're under attack. I think some of them are running away."

"What about us? They said that if the law found us they'd—"

"Stop it!" Willow snapped as she turned to look the young girl in the eyes. Keeping her gaze fixed on the girl, Willow lowered her voice to an intent whisper. "Nothing is going to happen to us. Isn't that right?"

Reflexively, the young girl glanced at the rest of the

prisoners, who were all trembling like leaves in the middle of an autumn wind. "That's right," she said unconvincingly.

Nodding, Willow said, "Those bastards are so worried about saving their own skins that they probably forgot about us. Can't you hear all that gunfire? It sounds like the Army is shooting cannons at them!"

"What if they shoot cannons at us?" asked a little boy curled into a ball on the floor. "We can't run anywhere."

Before Willow could think of something to say, she felt the door in front of her rattle against its hinges. The sudden noise caused her to jump back, which caused everyone else in the wagon to let out a few frightened yelps.

"Stay back," Willow said to the others. "If you see the chance to run, just take it."

"What are you going to do?"

"Don't think about that. If you see your chance, take it."

Willow crouched down in front of the door. The muscles in her legs tensed as she prepared to spring forward. The muscles in her arms and hands prepared to swing or claw at whatever she could reach. The muscles in the rest of her body prepared for the worst.

When the door finally came open, however, her entire body froze.

"Mason?" Willow said in disbelief. "Is that you?"

"Sure enough," Mason replied with a crooked grin. "You care to step out of there for a spell?"

Willow put her muscles to good use when she jumped out of the wagon and wrapped her arms around Mason's neck.

"Easy now, squaw. We ain't out of this yet. Not by a long shot." Mason lowered her from the wagon and set her down. Even after her feet had touched the ground, Willow wasn't quick to let him go.

"This is the second time you've taken me out of here," she said. "I can never thank you enough."

"If you want to thank me, take the rest of these folks

that's a way," Mason said while pointing to a path of low-hanging trees and tangled shrubs. "There's a small path that leads up to a dead end. If any of these other assholes see you headed there, run up to the top of the rocks using that trail there. They're done shooting up there for now. It ain't perfect, but it beats the hell out of staying in the open."

"I can help you gather up the rest of the prisoners," Willow offered as she waved for the others in the wagon to come out.

Mason shook his head. "No need. They're already waiting at the end of that path I showed you. All these guns were so busy trying to find me that they turned their back on where I'd snuck off to. Once I got down here, all I heard was the men rattling on about some band of marshals that was coming for them."

Smiling as she helped a few of the smaller children down from the wagon, Willow said, "When I turned myself in to Umberto, I told him there were U.S. marshals waiting to ambush him to the northwest."

"And he believed you?"

"It wasn't easy, but yes. He turned the wagons to the northeast."

"You did real good," Mason said. "Think you've got it in you to lead these folks to where they need to go?"

She nodded without hesitation.

"Good. Take this," he said while handing her a pistol. "Shoot anyone that tries to do you any harm. Me and Clint will come back for you before you know it."

Just as Mason was about to leave, he was stopped by Willow taking hold of him. She kissed him and gave him a hug. "Thank you so much."

"Yeah, yeah. Just get going." Once Willow and the rest of the prisoners were out of sight, he added, "Let's just hope this thing ends quick or it won't be pretty."

FORTY-FOUR

Clint turned on the balls of his feet, spotted his next target, and pulled his trigger. The longer he moved among the wagons, the fewer gunmen tried to stop him. Men were riding out of the canyon in both directions, shooting up toward the top of the ridge as if they could see lines of riflemen staring down at them.

By that time, Clint didn't even try to imagine what was going through their minds. His thoughts were centered on one target. All the others he gunned down were just bumps in the road.

"Umberto!" Clint shouted. "The only way out for you is through me!"

A shot cracked through the air and chewed off a piece of Clint's left arm. Acting on pure reflex, Clint twisted and returned fire. With that shot still ringing in his ears, he heard a familiar voice directly behind him.

Umberto was laughing. "I don't know who the hell you are," he snarled. "So I guess you get no name on your tombstone."

Clint froze in his spot. He could feel Umberto's aim focused on his back as if there was a hot poker jabbing between his shoulders. "This is about right for a piece-of-shit slave trader," Clint said. "Probably makes it easier to kill a man without seeing his face when it happens."

"You want me to see your face? All right then. Raise your arms high and turn around. I see that gun even twitch, and I kill you anyway."

Clint stuck his arms straight over his head and turned around slowly.

"Drop the gun," Umberto said, "and get on your knees."

Once again, Clint did as he was told. The moment the Colt was about to hit the dirt, Clint snapped his foot forward to kick the gun at Umberto.

The Mexican flinched and fired his shot, but his own twitching movements threw off his aim. Rather than give into the panic that had taken hold of his men, Umberto cleared his head quickly so his second shot would be on target.

By the time he had his eyes on Clint once more, Umberto saw the flicker of sharpened steel flying through the air. Clint's knife turned once after it had been thrown and then lodged into Umberto's chest. Stunned by the sudden stab of pain, Umberto didn't have time to realize what had happened before he was falling over. When he managed to suck in a breath and open his eyes, he saw Clint staring down at him.

Without saying a word, Clint turned away from the leader of the slavers so he could retrieve his Colt. Once that was done, he calmly walked away.

Umberto clawed at the ground as he struggled to pull himself up. The knife felt like a steel post nailing him to the ground, making it difficult for him to do anything but wheeze. Somehow, he managed to get himself propped up enough to see Clint walking off.

"Don't . . . turn your . . . back to me!" Umberto growled.

Clint kept walking.

Every one of Umberto's muscles were twitching inside him. He could feel them jumping around like snakes under his skin. If he tried to breathe too deeply, it felt as if the blade stuck inside him swelled to twice its size.

Finally, Umberto lifted his gun just enough to turn it toward Clint. He aimed at the other man and started the agonizing process of pulling the trigger.

The hammer of Umberto's pistol had just started to lift when Clint turned and sent a piece of hot lead through the slaver's skull. Umberto flopped facedown to the dirt. His eyes were still focused on his target.

FORTY-FIVE

Now that Umberto was a memory, Clint turned his attention to the rest of the slavers. Surprisingly enough, there weren't many of them left. Once he walked away from the burning wreckage and got somewhere away from the roar of flames, he found the men he was after.

Bunches of them were lying on the ground, wounded or dead. Even more of them were tied up in clusters of two or three, sitting on the ground with their heads hanging low.

"In the name of the law, lay down your guns and surrender!" came a booming voice.

Clint walked toward the source of the command. Although he lowered his pistol, he didn't let it leave his hand.

"The U.S. marshals have this area surrounded. Surrender or be shot!"

Clint took a few more steps, peering through the swirling mix of dust and smoke. "Mason? Is that you?"

The bounty hunter stepped forward, gave Clint a smirk, and said, "It's Marshall Glad to see you're alive, Adams." Mason stepped close enough so he could whisper to Clint without being heard by anyone else. "Willow got these boys believing the U.S. marshals were on their tails, so I figured why fight it?"

Clint nodded. "Where's the rest of these gunmen, Marshal?"

"Plenty got out of this canyon, but my men will round them up." When he saw the look on Clint's face, Mason nodded and shrugged. "But we got a good amount of them captured. As you'll see, plenty of them won't be drawing another lawless breath."

As he stepped past Mason, Clint whispered, "You already sold them. Don't overdo it."

"The prisoners are accounted for. I'd say we round up our own prisoners and get the hell out of here," Mason said, putting emphasis on the last six words.

Clint bent down to pick up a rifle that had been dropped during the fight. "All right, men," he said to the slavers tied up in front of him. "On your feet and head to one of those wagons."

As he rounded up the men that Mason had tied up, Clint found a few more that were too tired to fight and more than willing to take their chances with the law. Clint and Mason were almost at the entrance to the canyon when they got a look at the back portion of the caravan.

There were a few gaping holes left by the wagons that had been driven off at the first sign of trouble, but plenty more had been abandoned and left behind. Out of curiosity, Clint reached out to one of the wagons and pulled open the tarp. Inside, the wagon was stuffed full of blankets, food, and tools.

"Most of 'em are like that," Mason said. "I guess the ones that got away knew which wagons to take."

"What about the prisoners?" Clint asked. "Were they all accounted for?"

"If you mean the prisoners that were being hauled around like cattle, then yeah. They're all close by."

"That's all that matters." Clint stopped next to one of the empty wagons that had been used to transport the women and children the slavers had intended on selling. "Get in," Clint said to his own prisoners. It took a little doing, but the slavers climbed up into the wagon.

Before too long, Clint and Mason had filled two of the modified wagons with slavers. An hour later, they'd gathered up their horses, replenished their supplies, and were moving out of the smoke-filled canyon.

Clint drove a wagon that had been stripped of its tarp so the freed prisoners could ride in back with the sun on their faces. Eclipse followed alongside, welcoming the slower pace. Willow drove another wagon filled with the very same folks that she'd been locked up with for so long.

"Are we headed back into Sharps?" Willow asked.

"Only if that's where you want to go."

"Don't you need us to help you put those men away?"

Clint shook his head. "Mason's more than willing to take care of that. They're already wanted, so there's nothing much else you could do to them. Most of them will probably be hung the day after Mason hands them over."

"Where are you going?" Willow asked.

"To the closest train station. Mason's willing to use some of the reward money to pay to send you folks home."

"All of us?"

"All of you," Clint said with a tired smile.

"That's a lot of tickets to buy."

Clint looked over his shoulder and got a friendly, enthusiastic wave from Mason. "Those men are wanted dead or alive. I'd say that covering the price of a few train tickets won't be a problem." Turning back to face Willow, Clint added, "Or if anyone would rather ride off from here, there's still plenty of horses wandering around to choose from."

"I think we'll stay with you," Willow said. "We'd be safer that way."

"Sounds fine to me." With that, Clint snapped his reins and got the wagon moving.

Behind him, women and children who hadn't slept for days on end leaned back and closed their eyes. The ones who were too excited to sleep merely gazed up at the open sky. They tried not to look back at the wagons Mason was pulling. Those were full of enough dead slavers to feed a tub of worms for the rest of their lives.

When Mason looked back, all he saw was a gold mine.

Clint, on the other hand, was just glad to be headed somewhere for a change instead of chasing someone.

The road to hell was finally behind him.

Watch for

FAREWELL MOUNTAIN

294th novel in the exciting GUNSMITH series
from Jove

Coming in June!

GIANT WESTERNS FEATURING THE GUNSMITH

THE GHOST OF BILLY THE KID
0-515-13622-0

LITTLE SURESHOT AND THE WILD WEST SHOW
0-515-13851-7

DEAD WEIGHT
0-515-14028-7